DEVIL'S
CATACOMBS

Also by
Will Overby

The Island

The Killing Vision

The Human Condition:
Short Fiction and Poetry

Drum

August

DEVIL'S CATACOMBS

Will Overby

DAWSON SPRINGS, KENTUCKY
2014

This is a work of fiction. Names, characters, businesses, places, events and incidents are either the products of the author's imagination or used in a fictitious manner. Any resemblance to actual persons, living or dead, or actual events is purely coincidental.

Cover design by Kit Foster

ISBN-13: 978-0615972930
ISBN-10: 0615972934

PROLOGUE

In the cold darkness, in the depths where light had never shone and no living thing crept, it slumbered. It had not fed for some time, and now hunger was stirring it into consciousness, if such a being could be said to have consciousness. It had always been, and always would be, as long as other creatures existed to sustain it. Men had given it many names; some had worshipped it and some had concocted complicated rituals to drive it away. But all feared it. And in the end, it was the fear that gave it strength. Soon it would feed again and then return to its dark dreams to await the next cycle.

It never waited for long.

I
JARED

Jared Stone stepped out the back door of the sweltering restaurant kitchen into the cool October night, unbuttoning his shirt and letting the light breeze play over him. Friday nights at Antonio's were always crazy and this one had been no exception. Ever since he had come in at three, the place had been hopping. The restaurant closed at nine, but by the time the stragglers left, the last of the dishes were washed and put away, and the restrooms tidied up, it was usually eleven before he made it out. But tonight it was just ten-thirty. He had the next two days off and he was looking forward to spending them with Kassidy.

He climbed into his Accord and cranked the engine. Slipknot came blaring out of the speakers, making him jump. He reached over and turned it down as he wheeled through the parking lot, circling around the big green and white sign with the cartoon Italian man tossing a pizza, and pulled out into the Friday night traffic, heading toward Kassidy's apartment.

He and Kassidy had been together, what, two years now? Ever since they had been paired up as partners in astronomy lab during Jared's sophomore year. Hard to believe it had been that long, yet at other times it seemed the two of them had been dating forever. Kassidy was his first serious relationship since coming to college and he hoped it would be his last. He could totally see settling down with her and raising a family someday. House with a picket fence, couple of kids, all that shit. But that would be later. After he and Kassidy graduated and he had left the stinking hellhole that was Antonio's.

God, he hated that place. He hated handling strangers' dirty plates and the smell of rancid tomato sauce and the scuttle of black roaches in the corner by the dishwasher. He hated wiping crusted shit and piss off the bathroom walls, the pungent odor of the mop bucket, and he hated emptying the trash can in the foyer that always smelled like someone had thrown up in it. Most of all, he hated Denny, his shift manager. Denny was older, close to thirty, though with his receding hair and scraggly mustache he looked closer to forty. Denny always wore a long sleeve white shirt and a tie and called the customers "sir" and "madam." He called Jared "bud." As in, "Hey, bud, table four needs to be cleaned up pronto." Or, "Hey, bud, get that kitchen trash taken out before the coffee grounds leak all over the floor again." Denny was a dick. If this was still Lake County High School, Jared was sure he could round up a few of his football buddies and teach him a lesson.

But that was long ago and far away. Back before the

injury. Before the bone-splintering crack of that play in the third quarter that ended everything and left him with a bum knee that still gave him bouts of pain.

But he wouldn't think about that now. Tonight was all about having fun, tossing back a few drinks with his friends, maybe watching a movie. Hopefully spending the night with Kassidy.

He braked at a stop light and watched the traffic flow down the cross street. He and Kassidy had never made love in his bed, something he'd never considered and hadn't thought odd until now. In fact, she had never spent the night at his and Luke's apartment. Maybe she just wasn't comfortable there. He knew he and Luke weren't the neatest guys, and sure there was always a pile of dirty clothes in his bedroom floor and his bed was never made. And maybe his toilet needed a good scrubbing. But the place didn't stink, unlike some apartments in his complex. He should probably make an effort to be tidier, though. Girls didn't like clutter, even if it was clean clutter.

The light changed and he pulled through the intersection, passed the Cedar Hill College campus, then made a left onto Woodside. When Kassidy and her friend Chloe had first moved into their apartment in the old Victorian house, Jared was a little freaked out. This was the same building where the girl was murdered the previous summer. "You're being silly," Kassidy told him. "She lived upstairs. Not the same apartment. And they caught the woman who did it." Still, it took Jared several visits before the creepy feeling finally left him and he felt comfortable in the house. Superstition maybe, but he didn't think he could ever live in a place where someone had been killed.

He pulled up to a stop in front of the building. Luke's truck was already here, as were Kassidy's and Chloe's cars. No sign of Brandon's Mazda yet, but he was always the last to get here. Along the dark street the oaks rustled in the autumn wind and orange leaves scurried across the walk. A faint scent of wood smoke hung in the air. The light on the wide front porch burned warm and bright, and Jared realized he was chilly now that he was away from the hot kitchen, and he'd left his jacket in the car. No matter; he was still hoping he wouldn't be coming back outside until tomorrow morning.

The interior hall of the house was narrow and stuffy and smelled faintly of roses, and he could hear the chatter and the music before he reached Kassidy's door. Inside, the three of them were gathered around the small dining table, an open pizza box in front of them. Luke appeared to be on his second beer and Chloe was shooting him a narrow-eyed look over the top of her Dr Pepper can. Luke was laughing and holding a piece of half-eaten sausage pizza.

"What's up?" Jared said, closing the door behind him.

Chloe turned her dark eyes to him. "Nothing. Your roommate's just a jerk."

"Why? What happened?"

Chloe shook her head. "Not worth retelling."

Luke swallowed his bite of pizza and ran a hand through his spiky red hair. "Chloe was talking about the state fair back in Nebraska," he said in his Mississippi twang. "She said, and I quote, 'I always loved walking around the fair with a sack of hot nuts.'" He laughed harder and pounded a fist on the table.

Chloe slumped in her seat, and her dark skin seemed to have turned a shade of red. "Peanuts," she said. "Roasted peanuts."

Jared smacked Luke on the back of the head. "What are we, twelve years old?" He grabbed a slice of pizza and studied it before biting off the end. "This isn't from Antonio's is it?"

Kassidy gave him a crooked smile. "Papa John's."

Jared moved toward the refrigerator, still chewing. "I didn't think I could taste any roaches." He pulled a Mountain Dew from the shelf and popped the top.

"Yes," Kassidy said, blowing a tuft of blonde hair out of her eyes, "thanks to you and your stories I'll never eat at Antonio's again." She glanced at the clock on the microwave. "You're early. You didn't quit, did you?"

Jared took a swig from the can and washed down the pizza. "Unfortunately, no. Everyone just got their asses in gear tonight. Denny must've had a hot date." Jared and Kassidy locked glances and he thought he saw just a trace of a smile on her lips. It faded as quickly as it appeared, leaving him to wonder if he had seen it all. "Anyone heard from Brandon?"

Chloe picked up her phone. "He sent me a text half an hour ago. Said he'd be here by eleven."

Luke took a swig of beer. "Dude's gonna be late to his own fucking funeral."

Jared pulled out a chair and sat down at the table. "Somebody tell me why he's still living in the dorm."

"It's that Gutterman scholarship," Chloe said. "It won't pay for off-campus housing."

"I get that," Jared said, taking another bite of pizza. "But his parents aren't hurting for money. They could afford to put him up in an apartment."

"Less money they'd have for their own little toys," Chloe said, her lips curling in disgust. "And their trips everywhere." She waved her hand. "They're just ass-holes, both of them. They're the reason Brandon's ma-joring in finance, but he won't stand up to them."

"Brandon needs to grow a pair," Luke said.

"Yeah," Kassidy said, "like the two of you would tell off your parents if they were footing the bill for your college." She looked at Chloe. "Right, Miss Full-Ride Scholarship?"

"But they're *not* footing the bill," Chloe said. "Well, not all of it, anyway. You all just don't understand the situation. He's terrified of them. Especially his moth-er."

Luke arched his eyebrows. "Ooh, mommy issues."

Kassidy sighed. "Shut up, Luke." She looked at Chloe. "You ever met them?"

Chloe nodded. "Oh, yes. This semester on move-in day. His mom had apparently twisted somebody's arm to get Brandon his private room, and she was being a real bitch to the R.A., telling him he was not to enter the room without Brandon's permission and all kinds of stupid shit. Brandon's dad gave the front desk a busi-ness card and told them to give him a call personally if there was ever a problem, like Brandon was two years old or something. Poor Brandon just stood there the whole time like he wanted to sink through the floor. I was embarrassed for him." She sipped her Dr Pepper. "I was going to help carry some stuff up to the room, but Brandon's mom was like, 'No, we've got it, thanks.' Practically shoved me out the door."

"Wow," Kassidy said. "She really *is* a bitch."

"I think once Brandon graduates he's probably going to cut ties with them."

"Wow, I had no idea," Jared said.

Luke leaned back in his chair and eyed Chloe. "You know, you and Brandon sure are chummy," he said. "Makes me wonder if the two of you might have something going on the rest of us don't know about."

Chloe rolled her eyes. "We're just good friends," she said. "Besides, I don't have time for a boyfriend."

Luke sipped his beer. "Yeah, so you've told me."

Jared covered his mouth so Luke couldn't see his grin. Luke had been sniffing around Chloe since the five of them had started hanging out at the end of sophomore year. Jared had never really known what Chloe's deal was; they'd never seen her with another guy except Brandon, and she seemed content to be unattached. Luke, on the other hand, went through girls the way some guys went through socks. When Jared and Luke were still living in the dorm freshman year, Jared had spent many evenings in the library while Luke was getting busy in their room. It was a relief later to have Kassidy's room to retreat to, and an even bigger relief junior year to have a private room in an apartment. But the thin walls of the apartment couldn't filter out the sounds of Luke's activities, and Jared had learned to stick in his ear buds anytime Luke came through the door with a girl.

He glanced at Kassidy, hoping to share another knowing smile, but Kassidy wasn't looking at him. She was chewing her pizza and staring off into space. She had grown distant lately and he had wracked his brain trying to figure out what he might have done to offend her. He had just about decided he was imagining things, that maybe she was preoccupied with classes or her part-time job at Cato. After all, if something was wrong, she would tell him about it. Wouldn't she?

There was a soft knock at the door, and Brandon's goateed face appeared. "Hey, guys," he said.

"Where you been?" Luke said. "Flogging your log?"

Brandon flushed and pulled out of his jacket. "Any pizza left?" He was a big guy, almost six feet tall and weighing two-fifty easy, but gentle as a kitten, and Jared thought about the scene in the dorm Chloe had told them about.

Kassidy turned the box around. "Help yourself. Want a Coke?"

"Sure." Brandon sank into a chair and pulled out a slice. "How much do I owe?"

"Five bucks should cover it," Kassidy said. She pulled a can from the refrigerator and slid it across the table.

Brandon stuck the pizza in his mouth and pulled out his wallet. He slumped as he thumbed through it. He pulled the pizza from his mouth. "Can I get you next time?"

"I got it," Jared said, pulling out his own wallet and throwing a ten across the table to Kassidy.

"Thank you," Brandon said, taking a bite off the pizza. "I owe you." He gave Jared an apologetic smile.

"Don't worry about it," Jared said. He watched Brandon eat and wondered about the asshole parents that wouldn't even give their own kid pizza money.

"So," Brandon said, his mouth full, "I got something lined up I think you guys will like."

"If it involves beer and girls, I'm in," Luke said, tipping his bottle in Brandon's direction.

Brandon rolled his eyes. "Ever heard of Devil's Catacombs?"

Kassidy and Chloe shook their heads. "Sounds spooky," Chloe said.

"I know that place," Jared said. "Isn't that over by Indian Chief Cave?"

Brandon nodded. "Yeah, it's an offshoot of the cave. Supposed to have spectacular scenery, but it's not open to the public anymore."

"Wait a second," Kassidy said. "Is that the place where the people disappeared?"

"Yeah," Brandon said. He took another bite of pizza. "A few years back."

"I don't think I know this story," Luke said. "What do you mean, 'disappeared'?"

"They never found them, dude," Jared said. "Some guys went caving in there and never came out. Nobody knows what happened to them."

Luke looked at him. "Are you shitting me?"

"I shit you not, man," Jared said. "The place used to be open for tours, back when I was a little kid. The people that ran it went bankrupt or something and closed it. People used to sneak in there all the time and go exploring. Still do, I guess. I never did it, but I knew some guys back in high school that talked about it. Was supposed to be haunted or something."

"What?" Luke said. "How can a cave be haunted?"

Jared shook his head. "I don't know. Maybe an Indian's ghost or something. Who knows. Anyway, these guys went in and nobody ever heard from them again."

Luke smirked. "Bullshit."

"No, really," Jared said. "It was all over the news. Google it."

Brandon nodded and tore off another bite of pizza. "It's true," he said, his mouth full. "I remember hearing about it in high school."

"So what about this place?" Chloe said.

Brandon swallowed his bite of pizza. "How would you guys like to go there?"

Kassidy gaped at him. "To a haunted cave?"

"It'll be fun," Brandon said.

Chloe was shaking her head. "This girl doesn't go into any kind of cave. Haunted or not."

Luke grinned at her. "I'll protect you."

Jared frowned. "I don't know, Brandon. Sounds dangerous."

"No, no," Brandon said, holding up his hands. "I've got it all worked out. There's this guy, Kyle. He says he's been in there dozens of times. He's an experienced caver."

"*We're* not experienced cavers," Chloe said.

"We don't have any kind of equipment," Jared said.

"Kyle's got it all," Brandon told them. "Ropes, knee pads, lights, the works. He'll outfit us and take us in and show us around. We'll just need to bring backpacks with our own water and snacks."

Luke looked at him. "So who is this guy?"

"I met him through work," Brandon said.

"At the financial aid office?" Chloe said.

"Yeah."

Jared plucked a ball of sausage off the remaining pizza and tossed it in his mouth. "So he's a student."

"Potential student," Brandon said. "He just got out of the army. He's a little older than us, around thirty, I think. Wants to major in geology."

"Wait," Kassidy said, "so you just met this guy and he agreed to take us all on a little jaunt through the cave?"

Brandon shrugged and his cheeks reddened. "Yeah."

"All of us?"

"Yeah." He looked at each of them. "What's wrong? I thought everyone would be excited to do something besides get drunk and watch bad movies all night."

"How do you know this dude's not gonna rob us or something?" Luke said.

"He's cool," Brandon said. "I've talked to him several times. He's been in and out of the office over the past few weeks trying to get something settled with his G.I. Bill for the spring semester. His family owns a big sporting goods store over in Springfield. Young Brothers, I think."

Jared nodded. He knew the place well. It took up a whole city block downtown and had always been the main supplier for Lake County's sports teams. "So he's part of the Young family?"

Brandon nodded and took a long swig of his Coke. "Really great guy. You all will like him. I think he just wants some friends."

Luke peeled off a corner of the label on his beer. "So when are you thinking about doing this?"

"How about Sunday? No one's working, right?"

They all looked at each other.

Luke took a gulp of beer and set his bottle down with a thud. "I don't know about the rest of these asswipes, but I'm all for it."

"I'm off all weekend," Jared said. He looked at Kassidy. "I know you're off Sunday."

She shrugged. "I'm not saying I'll go." She glanced at him and gave him a surrendering frown. "I guess we can do it." She smiled thinly, and Jared knew this wasn't something she wanted to do.

Brandon looked at Chloe. "Come on. Don't be the only holdout."

"I don't like caves," Chloe said, her dark eyes flashing. "And it sounds illegal."

"People go in there all the time," he said. "And Kyle will be with us."

Luke put an arm around her. "I won't let anything happen to you," he said.

She grabbed his hand and pulled it off her. "Give me a break."

"I know how you feel," Kassidy said. "Caves are scary places. It's the dark. There could be anything in there."

"It's not really the dark I'm scared of," Chloe said, glancing at Luke.

Luke looked at her, a sly smile on his lips. "So what *are* you afraid of, Chloe?"

Jared took a swig of Mountain Dew. "You know what I'm afraid of? Snakes." He pictured a slimy python slithering through the grass and felt a shudder.

"That's true," Kassidy said. "We went to the zoo once and Jared wouldn't even go into the reptile house." The others laughed.

Jared snorted. "Why don't you tell them what *you're* afraid of, Kassidy?"

She slumped. "Dogs."

Luke turned. "Big dogs?"

"Any dogs. I'm terrified of them." She held up her hand and pointed to a triangle-shaped scar just above her wrist. "I got bit by my aunt's German shepherd when I was five. Stitches, rabies shots in the stomach, the whole nine yards. It was horrible."

"I don't like heights," Luke said. "I'm scared of falling. I can't even go up a ladder at the paint store without getting dizzy."

"You're not dizzy," Kassidy said, "you're probably just drunk."

Brandon had pulled out his phone and was frantically texting. "I'll tell Kyle it's a go. He'll be excited." He stopped and looked at them. "It *is* a go, right?"

Jared and Luke nodded. "Sounds fun," Jared said.

Chloe leaned back in her chair. "Count me in for the moment. Not saying I won't change my mind."

Beside Jared, Kassidy sighed and grabbed a DVD off the counter. "Who's ready for a movie?"

2
KASSIDY

Kassidy stirred in the early morning light and felt Jared's warmth beside her.

She lay staring at the ceiling, thinking about how she had let him talk his way into staying the night. She had told herself she wasn't doing this anymore. That she was going to start weaning him away from her. Then, last night when the movie was over and Brandon and Luke had gone and Chloe had retreated to her room, Jared looked at her with those soft blue eyes and she felt something give way in her chest. And suddenly she wanted him, wanted to be on top of him, moving with him. He led her toward her room and she followed like a lamb to slaughter. And when it was over and he was curled against her, breathing the steady rhythm of sleep, she lay in the darkness watching the shadows of the trees claw across the ceiling and wondering what the fuck she was going to do.

She had felt herself slipping away from him little by

little over the past few months. At first she began noticing how little the two of them had in common. Then
things began to irritate her, like the way he sometimes
snorted when he laughed. She had thought it was cute
when they first started dating, but now it was just gross.
She had come close to breaking things off at the beginning of summer when they were both working more
and seeing each other less. It would have been easy
then to come up with excuses. But now the gang was
all back together, and cutting off Jared would mean the
end of all of them. And she didn't think she could do
that right now.

The truth was, she had fallen for Luke. She loved
his Southern drawl and decent manners, and he reminded her of the boys back home in Texas. He certainly
had the charm. And it was his charm that had lured her
into his bed one night when she had shown up at his
and Jared's apartment to wait for Jared to get off work.
They certainly hadn't meant for it to happen. They'd
been sitting on the couch, watching Daniel Tosh and
laughing together, and suddenly they realized their
hands were touching. One look at each other was all it
took, and then they were wrapped up together, devouring each other. The next thing she knew they were going at it between Luke's freshly-laundered sheets. Luke
was moaning, and that excited her to the point of slipping over the edge. And when it was over and they
were once again planted on opposite ends of the couch
in front of the TV, they swore they would never talk
about what happened, even to each other. Jared would
be devastated, and even though she knew she was losing her feelings for him, she couldn't do that to him.
She wasn't cruel.

But sometimes, like now, she wished she was waking up with Luke. That it was his muscled arms and tousled red hair peeking out of the covers. She had told herself it was a one-time thing, and deep down she knew it. But she caught herself at times gazing too long into Luke's eyes or letting her hand linger on his shoulder. And she wondered if he ever felt it, too.

But that was crazy. Luke was in love with Chloe, they all knew that. Even Chloe. And Kassidy couldn't understand why Chloe was constantly giving him the brush-off. She did like him – it was obvious in the way she laughed at his jokes and bantered with him. At first Kassidy wondered if it was because Chloe was African-American and Luke was white, and if this was 1965 she might have accepted that. But it was the twenty-first century. Mixed-race couples weren't out of the ordinary any longer. No, Kassidy had decided that Chloe wanted Brandon. And why not? They were both quiet and studious and seemed to enjoy many of the same things. The problem was, Brandon didn't seem to realize it. Chloe was definitely going to have to make the first move if that relationship was ever going to get a kick-start. It was like watching a suspense movie, seeing what the heroine needed to do and screaming at the screen even though you knew she couldn't hear you.

Kassidy sighed and turned over to check her clock. 7:45. She didn't have to be in to work until ten. If she got on up now, maybe she could get in a quick read of that chapter in Childhood Development, since she wouldn't get a chance tomorrow like she'd planned. She was so tired of school. Some days it was all she could do to drag herself to class and listen to one more lecture, take one more test, write one more paper. Next semester she would be student teaching, and she couldn't wait. She had dreamed of teaching little kids since middle school, when she had worked as a student aid for Mrs. Murphy's third-grade class. She loved kids, and they all seemed to love her, and she couldn't imagine a better career than being an elementary teacher. But to get there, she was going to have to make it through two more semesters.

No, actually a semester and a half now. She had to keep reminding herself of that.

She sat up and swung her legs off the side of the bed. Behind her, Jared stirred and reached for her. "What time is it?" he said.

"Almost eight."

"You want to go get some breakfast?"

"Not really. I need to study a little before I get ready for work."

"Okay."

"I'll make you some coffee."

"That's all right. I'll stop by the Java Station on my way home." He rubbed his hand across her back and his fingers felt like sandpaper.

"You sure?"

"Yeah." She felt him roll toward her and his hands encircled her waist. He kissed the small of her back. "One day we'll get to wake up and I won't have to leave."

"Yeah," Kassidy said, staring at the wall. "That'll be nice."

3
CHLOE

Chloe set down her worn paperback and listened to the voices pass by in the hall. Jared and Kassidy. She sighed. Sometimes Kassidy was a real bitch. Chloe wondered when she was going to stop stringing Jared along and set him free. It wasn't right. Everyone knew it. Everyone could see it except poor deluded Jared. And Chloe was not going to be the one to point it out to him.

She heard the front door close and sat up. She took off her reading glasses and stretched, feeling the stiffness in her neck. She'd been awake for hours reading. A crime novel by Karin Slaughter she'd saved from the discard pile in the library. It was good to have perks at work, chief among them the opportunity to go through books that were being culled from the stacks and donation bins. The campus library didn't house much contemporary fiction, so when contribution boxes came in, those were usually the first to be thrown out. It made her sad to see heaps of books being trashed, and sadder still for the people who felt the need to get rid of them in the first place.

Reading had been her main source of entertainment growing up. Her family had moved at the beginning of middle school so her father could open his own dental practice, and it had been a tough year for her. For starters, she was the only African American out of thirty kids in her sixth grade class. And while that wasn't such a big deal in a town like Lincoln, Nebraska, it still made her feel awkward and lonely. She got glasses right after Christmas, and that, coupled with her excellent grades, cemented her reputation as one of the smart kids. Teachers loved her. Other kids considered her a goody-two-shoes. So she did the only thing she could – she escaped into a world of books. She'd started out with middle-grade novels but it wasn't long before she graduated to more mature works by Stephen King and Toni Morrison. By seventh grade she'd earned special permission to check out books from the high school library. But it wasn't just the stories she loved. It was the books themselves. The heft of them, the feel of smooth paper beneath her fingertips, the smells of ink and glue and time. Heaven, if it existed, would be constructed of towers of books and she would have eternity to read them all.

When she had come to Cedar Hill, part of her scholarship to the small liberal arts college included employment, and by some miracle she'd been given the opportunity to work in the library. Never did she feel more alive than when she was cataloging or shelving books, which she knew made her somewhat of an anomaly to her co-workers, who avoided those jobs at all costs. But her willingness to accept lowly tasks put her in good graces with Rita, the circulation supervisor, and resulted in better hours, less supervision, and this semester, a jump in pay. She wondered at times if she should change her major from sociology to library science, even if she had to go to a different university, but talks with Rita had convinced her that employment opportunities along with the pay scale would not be worth it. Besides, she hoped one day to teach sociology at the college level, so she planned to never stray far from academia and the books she so loved.

She glanced at the clock. She was scheduled for noon to seven today, and had planned to use her day off tomorrow to do some studying for a mid-term. But now that Brandon had come up with the bright idea to visit Devil's Catacombs, that was shot.

Unless she could talk her way out of going. She'd always hated caves. It wasn't that she was claustrophobic, but the idea of all that rock and earth above was terrifying, the immense weight hanging over your head and held up only by the sheer will of God. But she hated to disappoint Brandon. He'd apparently gone to great lengths to plan this venture out, and she didn't want to be a killjoy. She of all people. His best friend.

She'd first met Brandon in the financial aid office when she was a scared doe-eyed freshman trying to match up her tuition bill with her scholarship money. Something wasn't working out, and while she was waiting to speak with a counselor, a big teddy bear of a guy offered her a soda while she sat on the bench. He was a student worker there, it turned out. A sophomore, and the first person in the office to show any kind of true concern for her. She'd started crying. It was all so overwhelming and complicated and it was the first time she'd ever felt stupid in her life. Brandon sat with her and helped her calm down, and by the time her name was called, she was feeling confident again. And when she emerged after straightening everything out, he had been gone. And she had been surprisingly disappointed. But when she spotted him in her Intro to English Lit class, she made a bold move to go up and talk to him. Yes, he remembered her, and he hoped things were going well. No, he didn't have a girlfriend, and sure, grabbing a quick soft drink together in the student lounge sounded great.

They talked forever. About books, about school, about being only children, about their parents. His mother was a bank president back home in Evansville, Indiana. His father was a realtor. And while they seemed an important part of his life, none of them were especially close. His mother seemed downright cruel at times. Her idea of sending Brandon off to college had consisted of providing him with a car to get there and letting him figure out the rest on his own. By outward appearances Brandon had taken it all in stride and flourished under the pressure, but Chloe could tell he was deeply resentful of his parents' abandonment.

After that, they began seeing each other more often, occasionally having lunch together and hanging out or going to the movies when they both had some time off. At first Chloe thought a romance was blossoming, and that terrified her. She had never had a boyfriend, and the idea of being intimate with someone was both repulsive and intriguing. But as time passed, she realized they were enjoying just being good friends, and that was fine with her. Brandon was like a big brother, loving and protective. She certainly couldn't deny that she felt safer when she was with him. And she didn't want to risk their friendship by pushing for a romantic relationship. Besides, if she wanted a boyfriend, Luke was always available.

Luke. Now there was a case. She couldn't for the life of her understand why he kept after her when she had never given him any indication she was remotely interested in him. Not that he wasn't nice to look at. Red hair and freckles weren't her thing, but he had a good body and bright green eyes that seemed to know what she looked like without her clothes on. But he wasn't her type. He was too much of a partier and way too experienced for her. No, if she ever decided to pursue anyone, she hoped to find another virgin like herself. Which she was almost sure Brandon was.

She pulled on a pair of jeans and a clean sweatshirt and made her way down the hall to the kitchen. Kassidy was sitting at the table reading a textbook with a bottle of water beside her. "Did we wake you?" Kassidy asked, not looking up.

"No," Chloe said. "I was reading."

Kassidy motioned to her book. "Yeah, I hear you." She flipped through the pages. "I was hoping to get through this chapter before work since I probably won't get to read it tomorrow."

Chloe flopped down in chair. "Are you really going?"

Kassidy frowned and closed her book, marking her place with a finger. "I don't know. I don't really like caves. It would be something to do, though, I guess."

Chloe looked at her. "Cut the shit, Kassidy."

"What?"

"How much longer are you going to keep playing Jared?"

Kassidy sighed and set the book down, then reached for her water. "I don't know what to do, Chloe. It will kill him if I break things off. Just kill him."

Chloe frowned. "You aren't doing him any favors, you know."

"I know." Tears formed in her eyes. "It's just so damn hard. I still care about him, you know?"

"I understand."

"But I just don't. . . *love* him anymore."

"I get that," Chloe said. "But the thing is, he still loves you. The longer you let this go, the worse it's going to be. For the both of you."

"Yeah, I know." She wiped her eyes. "Maybe . . ."

"What?"

Kassidy stared at her book and traced a finger around the smiling gap-toothed child on the cover. "Maybe tomorrow night. After we get back from the cave and everyone else is gone."

"I can make myself scarce," Chloe said.

Kassidy nodded. "I'd like that. I appreciate it."

"No problem."

"And Chloe . . ."

"Yes?"

"Don't say anything to anyone. Not even Brandon."

Chloe nodded and turned an imaginary key on her lips.

4
LUKE

Luke tapped the horn of his Tacoma at the blue Malibu in front of him. The light was green. Why the fuck wasn't she going? The driver caught his eye in her rear-view mirror and glared at him. Well, she could eat him. He was going to be late for work and he didn't have time to be jacking around in traffic. An Aldean song came on the radio, and he cranked the volume up. "Dirt Road Anthem." God, he loved this song. He could get through anything while this song was playing. He caught sight of an opening in the traffic and raced to fill it.

He'd worked at Parker Paint for a year now. Mr. Parker was good guy, always willing to work around Luke's class schedule. And he liked Luke. Because Luke did his job and didn't complain and he wasn't a slacker like the little high school punks who came in on weekends and were constantly texting their girlfriends from the back storage room. Mr. Parker saw potential

in him. He had told him so. And he had made no secret of the fact that Luke would be his first choice to
take over as manager next year after graduation, if Luke
wanted to stay. Mr. Parker planned on retiring and
turning over the running of the business. "None of my
kids got any interest in paint," Mr. Parker told him.
"But you get it. You got a good head for the business,
and you know what it takes to keep up with Lowe's and
Walmart."

Indeed he did. And what he knew was nothing he
had learned in his business classes. It was knowing the
customers and what they needed. It was courting the
building contractors and giving them special deals and
making them feel like they were the most important cli-
ents the store had. That kind of thing built loyalty.
And even if Parker's couldn't price match every time,
personal service still went a long way in this town. It
was a business – a career – he could see himself doing
for a long time. And possibly, one day in the future, he
could buy out Mr. Parker and own the store outright.
But before he could own the business, he had to get
there on time.

He was scheduled to close the store at five, and after
that he thought he might get cleaned up and head down
to the old Capitol Theatre, which was now a dance club.
He hated the music they played there – a mixture of
Top Forty and trance shit – but it was a good place to
pick up women. Most of the girls that frequented the
Capitol were under thirty, and though the atmosphere
and the drinks were better at the bars on the outskirts of
town, the women there were older and broken down
and not worth looking at. He preferred his meat tender
and tight.

Jared wasn't working tonight, and Luke wished he could talk him into coming along. But Jared was so far up Kassidy's ass he couldn't see what she was doing to him. She was going to break up with him, and it wouldn't be long now. And when it happened, it would be the end of Jared's world.

Luke knew sleeping with Kassidy had been a mistake. She knew it, too. A spontaneous act they would probably regret the rest of their lives. For a while he was terrified Kassidy would tell Jared; after all, what better way to get rid of your boyfriend than tell him you slept with his best friend? But Kassidy had apparently not said a word and Jared continued to live in ignorance. Luke and Kassidy never talked about what happened that night, but sometimes he caught her looking at him, and he wondered if she still thought about what they might have had together.

But hot as Kassidy was, it was Chloe that turned his crank. He thought he could easily fall in love with her. He loved the way she smiled when she thought no one was looking at her and the melodic lilt in her voice when she laughed. He loved her dark eyes and her perfect teeth and the way she bit her bottom lip when he teased her and she was irritated. Most of all he loved the air of innocence she carried about her and he wondered, not for the first time, whether she was a virgin. It was a thought that made him want her more, and a thought that kept him awake sometimes at night, hot and sweating in his bed. They were thoughts that were still frowned on back home in Mississippi, and he wondered what his dad would say if he found out his son had the hots for a black girl.

Yes, good old John Robert Hartley, principal of

Robert Lowry High School and the reason Carrie Anderson, a fresh-faced English teacher, had to resign during her first year. The story had been kept hushed up, but Luke, still in middle school at the time, heard plenty of accusations flying about through his parents' closed bedroom door. There was talk of a ride home that had ended not at Carrie Anderson's front door but in the parking lot of a Super 8 motel just outside of Jackson. There was talk of pregnancy, and an abortion, and threats of divorce. It was the kind of talk no thirteen-year-old boy needed to hear, the kind of talk that made Luke feel hollow inside. The kind of talk that drove him to choose a college five hundred miles away from a home he never wanted to return to.

He hoped Chloe would go with them tomorrow. Even if she and Brandon were an item, which was something Luke could never quite figure out, he couldn't imagine that relationship working out. He only hoped that when Chloe realized it she would be ready to land right in Luke's arms for some sympathy. And he would be more than willing to give it.

5
BRANDON

Brandon checked his phone for the tenth time in thirty minutes. Kyle had promised to text him tonight to confirm everything was still on for tomorrow. It was almost eleven now, and still he had heard nothing.

What a day this had been. It started at six when some damn fool decided to wake the entire floor by running up and down the hall screaming, "Yikes and away!" Hearing a Daffy Duck cartoon quoted at such an ungodly hour was not exactly the best way to start the day, and by the time things were quiet again, Brandon was fully awake and knew he could never get back to sleep. He made his way down the hall to take a shower, and when he returned to his room he realized he had forgotten his key. He hadn't done that since freshman year, when he'd been locked out wearing only a towel. Today at least he still had his sleep pants and a t-shirt with him. Downstairs the pimply-faced front desk clerk was severely irritated that work on his latest production on Vine was being interrupted to go let Brandon into his room. What a little prick. It was then Brandon discovered he was out of breakfast food, and he couldn't go to the cafeteria because on Saturday they didn't start serving until ten. And he couldn't go grab anything at a restaurant because he was completely out of money. He ended up scarfing down the rest of a bag of Funyuns and an orange soda. Yep. Breakfast of champions.

At ten he called his mother to ask her to put more money into his bank account and apparently interrupted her treadmill workout. "What do you mean, more money?" she said. "I just put five hundred in there yesterday."

Crap. He hadn't even thought to look online at his account. "Sorry," he said. "I didn't know."

"You really should check these things, Brandon," his mother told him. "You've got to be more responsible."

"I know. I'm sorry."

"And for God's sake, stop going through this money like water. What are you spending it all on?"

"Gas. Food." Hell, she looked at his account every day in her office. She should know he wasn't being frivolous.

"I would think you'd get enough food on campus without having to go anywhere else. What's with all the debit card transactions at that Mexican restaurant?"

He sighed. "I just need a break from the cafeteria sometimes, Mom. And I like to go out with my friends occasionally."

"Well, this five hundred should last you the rest of the semester. Don't blow it all in a week."

"I won't." *Jesus.* "Is Dad around?"

"He's showing a house. Saturdays are usually busy for him."

"Yeah, I know. I just thought maybe – "

"People work during the week, Brandon. Most of them can only meet with him on evenings and week-ends."

"I know that. I just wondered if he was there."

"Mid-terms are next week, aren't they?"

Oh, here we go. "Yes. I've been studying."

"I was looking at your grades the other day. You've got to do better than a C in Experimental Economics."

"It's a hard class. Even the prof says it's a difficult subject."

"You've got to maintain that scholarship."

"I know. I'm trying."

There was a moment of silence. "Well, I've got to go," she said. "I'm standing here dripping sweat all over the floor."

Ew. "All right. I'll talk to you later. Thanks for putting the money in the account."

"You're welcome. Love you." The phone clicked and she was gone.

He sat staring at the screen for a moment. He should really start using cash more. Then at least she couldn't watch every penny he was spending. And it wasn't like he was frittering away his money on booze and parties. He really didn't understand her. Half the time she pushed him to be more independent, and the other half she dictated what he needed to do. There was no win-ning with her. At least now he could go stock up on a few things at Walmart, maybe grab a bite of real food while he was out.

The October sun was bright and hot, and as he

pulled out of the parking lot he spotted two guys going for a run along the sidewalk that bordered the quad. They were shirtless and chiseled, and he watched them until they disappeared, even though they weren't his type. And he was sure he wasn't theirs. They were too skinny. Too hairless. Too perfect. And most likely, too straight.

He made it to Walmart, picked up a few necessities and on a whim grabbed a package of Oreos and a half gallon of vanilla ice cream. If he couldn't find love at least he could enjoy a good snack. And ice cream was almost as good as sex anyway. Or so he'd heard the ladies in the office say.

He'd always known he was different, even as a little kid in daycare. When everyone was playing house, he'd always wanted to be the mom. No, not the mom. Another dad. Why couldn't a house have two dads instead of a dad and mom? None of the other kids wanted to bend the rules of the game for him, and none of the other boys wanted to play the other dad, so most often he was left to play alone. Sometimes he played with Gretchen, a girl with a bowl haircut, and she would pretend to be a boy. He often wondered about Gretchen, and whether she had grown up to be a lesbian.

As he got older, he began to understand that not only was he gay, but according to what he was hearing in the Catholic Church he was also doomed to eternal damnation. He was terrified, and he spent many sleepless nights praying and agonizing over these desires that he neither had control of nor truly wanted to go away. It was not anything he could discuss with anyone, even in confession. Especially in confession. He spent his high school years talking with other guys about girls and sex, but secretly lusting after the more muscular members of the school's football team. No one ever suspected he was gay, and he worked hard to keep it that way. He could only imagine what kind of living hell he would endure if his parents ever found out.

When Kyle Young had first entered the financial aid office that hot day in August, Brandon had all but melted to the floor. Kyle was a strapping six feet with a dark bushy goatee and a wolf tattooed on his forearm and smelled like heaven. Something expensive, not Axe like all the guys in the dorm seemed to bathe in. He and Brandon struck up an immediate conversation. Brandon learned that Kyle was fresh out of the army – ten years as an enlisted man including two tours of duty in Iraq. Suddenly back in civilian life, he was struggling to find his place and thought he might take advantage of his G.I. Bill and go back to school. Kyle's family owned a big sporting goods store over in Springfield, but he had no desire to go into the business. He was considering majoring in geology, something he'd always been interested in, and what did Brandon think? Flustered, Brandon mumbled something about a person following his dreams and Kyle heartily agreed. After that, Kyle became somewhat of a regular in the financial aid office, and he always made a point to stop and talk to Brandon. For a while, Brandon wondered if Kyle was coming on to him, especially after they exchanged phone numbers, but he finally became painfully aware that Kyle was just in search of new friends. All his old classmates from high school had either moved away or were married and had kids; none of his army mates lived anywhere close by. He was lonely and wanted someone to hang out with. Still, Brandon kept the hope that their friendship could grow into something else, and that he would finally have someone to truly share his life with. And, of course, someone to take his virginity. They'd gone hiking together over at the lake in September, something Brandon had kept from Chloe because he was afraid she might be jealous. It was on that excursion that Kyle had talked about wanting to get married and have a family someday, and Brandon knew that Kyle was out of his reach. It was sobering and depressing, and he knew he had been a fool for even thinking about such things.

He checked his phone. It was after eleven now. He couldn't stand it any longer. He texted to Kyle, *Everything still on for tomorrow?* And then he waited.

After a couple of minutes, his phone vibrated in his hand. A message back from Kyle. *Yeh. Meet u in parking lot @ store @ 11.*

Store? What store? He keyed back, *Young's???*
Yeh.

Whatever. "Yes" was the appropriate word. *Was wondering about you*, Brandon wrote. *Thought you forgot.*

After a moment the phone buzzed. *Sorry. Had a date and fell asleep.*

Brandon blew out a breath. A date. He felt a wave of disappointment and immediately stopped himself. It wasn't like Kyle had dumped him or anything. It wasn't like he'd been stood up for the eighth grade dance. Actually, he was glad for Kyle, glad he had managed to find someone. But he couldn't help hating that it wasn't him. His thumbs pecked out on the keyboard, *See you tomorrow*, then he tossed the phone to the side.

Immediately, he picked it back up. He needed to text everyone else and let them know the trip was still on.

6
JARED

The day dawned cold and rainy, and when his phone beeped at nine Jared thought he must be mistaken. It had to be earlier, like six. Thick gray clouds covered the sun, and when he finally stood at his bedroom window and peeked through the blinds he could see a steady drizzle falling on the parking lot below. Nice day for a drive.

The plan was for the five of them to drive to Springfield and meet up with Brandon's friend Kyle, then head out toward Indian Chief Cave. It would be at least an hour drive from Springfield, maybe longer. After going through the cave, they would head back home, maybe stopping for something to eat on the way.

Jared wasn't looking forward to being cooped up in the car with Kassidy all that time. Something was definitely going on with her. He could feel it, like a thickness in the air. Last night he'd called her around seven, when she would just be getting home from work, thinking maybe they could grab dinner, maybe a late movie. But she'd begged off. "I'm really tired," she said. "And I need to rest up if we're gonna be tromping through a cave all day tomorrow."

"How about I just come over?" he said. "I could stop by a drive-through and bring you something to eat."

"I don't think so. Not tonight." And he could hear an air of finality in her tone.

"All right," he said. "Whatever. You sure you want to go tomorrow?"

"Sure," she said. "It'll be fun."

"You don't sound very enthused."

She sighed. "What do you want me to do, Jared? Jump up and down and squeal? It's a fucking cave."

And now he watched the steady rain outside the window and wondered what he could have done to piss her off. He'd always tried to be attentive, tried to be considerate. He wasn't an asshole, not like some guys he knew. And then a thought struck him. Could she be interested in someone else? Was she seeing some other guy on the side? But that was ridiculous. Kassidy wasn't the kind to do that. There had to be something else wrong with her.

He eased back onto the bed and massaged his knee. This cooler weather was making it hurt like fuck. He bent his leg, then stretched it out. Six weeks on crutches and another two months of physical therapy and no one could tell him why his knee still gave him fits. The thought that he would have to endure this intermittent pain for the rest of his life both depressed and angered him. He was young. He shouldn't have the knee of a seventy-year-old man.

He had been on track for a football scholarship from the University of Georgia when the accident happened. In fact, an assistant Bulldogs coach was seated in the stands that night, waiting to meet with Jared and his parents after the game. He was thrilled. It was his second year as quarterback, and he had led the Tigers through a lossless season so far. And the game was going well. Lake County was ahead of Butler by fourteen and Lake County had possession. There were forty-five seconds left in the third quarter and they were fifteen yards from the end zone. It was going to be a piece of cake to make the touchdown. The play was all in his head. Kerry Robinson would snap the ball to him. Jared would fake a left, then rush right. By that time Chad Blakely would be in the end zone, ready to receive. Jared would throw the ball, Chad would grab it. Touchdown. But something happened. Kerry snapped the ball and Jared grabbed it. Moved left. Stepped right. Looked for Chad. But Chad wasn't there. No one was there. All Jared saw was a sea of maroon uniforms rushing him. He raised his arm to pass the ball out of bounds to stop the play and that's when the pain in his knee took him down. Unrelenting, paralyzing pain. A Butler lineman had landed on Jared's outstretched leg, and the leg was bent at an impossible angle. Whistles were blowing and the other players were suddenly crowded around him. But it was all hazy and muted. At some point he passed out, and the next thing he could remember was waking up in an ambulance on the way to the hospital and seeing his mother looking at him with tears in her eyes. After a few agonizingly boring days in the hospital, Jared returned to school on crutches. Everyone was calling him "Joe Theisman" and joking about the similarities of their injuries. But after a few weeks Jared knew the truth. His football career was over. No Georgia scholarship. No more dreams of maybe someday going pro. It was done.

He rubbed his knee and stared at the gray light through the blinds. In a few months he would be graduating with a degree in marketing and no fucking clue what he would do after that. Up until now life after college had seemed like a faraway dream with no reason for concrete goals and no real aspirations. But now it was looming before him like a brick wall. He would get a real job, have a real life and try to figure out where he was going. As much as he wanted to be done with school and out of Antonio's he had to admit that the future was frightening. Responsibility sucked.

There was a light knock on the door, and Luke said, "Jared, you up?"

"Yeah, come on in."

Luke peeked around the door. "We need flashlights or anything?"

Jared pulled a clean t-shirt from a pile in the laundry basket and slipped into it. "Brandon said Kyle's providing everything."

Luke shrugged. "I think I'll put one in my backpack. Just in case."

"Whatever."

Luke looked at him. "You okay, man?"

Jared nodded. He wasn't in the mood to chat. "Just tired."

"I hear you, dude. Too fucking early."

"What time you get in last night?"

Luke tried to hide a grin. "*We* got in about one." He cocked his head toward the front of the apartment.

"She just left."

Jared shook his head. Jesus. "Whatever. Let me get dressed and we'll go pick up everybody."

7
KASSIDY

Kassidy was just stirring from a disjointed dream about losing her way in the endless hallways of her high school when Jared's ringtone brought her fully awake. She looked at the phone. 9:15. *Shit*. She'd forgotten to set an alarm. "Hello?"

"Hey," Jared said. "We're getting ready to head out. You still going?"

Kassidy pulled a strand of hair out of her eyes. God, she didn't want to do this. Not the cave, not the drive. Not Jared. She didn't even know if she could take Luke today. But she had told everyone she would go. She'd even posted something about it on Facebook last night.

"Kassidy?"

"Yeah, I'm going," she said. "I overslept."

Jared was silent for a moment. "If you don't want to go, you don't have to."

God, she hated when he patronized her. "I know I don't have to go," she said. "I told you I would go, and

I will."

"Okay, don't get all pissy. What about Chloe? Is she going?"

"As of last night she was. I haven't talked to her yet this morning."

"Well, we'll be there in about fifteen minutes. We're going to pick up Brandon first."

"I'll be ready," she said.

She hung up and dragged herself out of bed. She was just going to have to power through this. She should have let him come over last night. She could have ended it then. Why did she agree to go to this stupid cave? Now she would have to dread their conversation all day. It was going to be bad.

The last bad breakup she'd had was in high school, right after senior prom. She and Marc had been together for three years, and though they both knew it was coming, it was still difficult. He accused her of cheating on him (she hadn't), and she told him she didn't love him anymore (even though she did). By the time the screaming and shouting was over, they were holding each other, both of them crying. But they knew it was over.

This would be worse than that. Because this time she *had* cheated, and this time she really *had* fallen out of love. And if Jared found out she had slept with Luke. . . well, as her grandmother back in Plano would say, that would be all she wrote.

Chloe was reading at the kitchen table when Kassidy came out of her room. She looked up from her book. "You're going?"

Kassidy gave her a tight smile. "Are you?"

Chloe put her book down. "You know, I figured,

why not. I'm always pushing myself to try new things. And I don't want to disappoint Brandon."

Kassidy grabbed a Coke from the refrigerator. "I thought you didn't like caves."

"I don't, but it's not a phobia or anything. It's just not something I would choose over say, eating cheese-cake."

Kassidy laughed and sat down at the table. "They're on their way. Jared just called me."

Chloe looked at her. "Still having the talk tonight?"

Kassidy nodded. She felt her eyes welling up, and she blinked back the tears. "This is going to be so damned hard, Chloe."

8

CHLOE

The guys arrived a little after 9:30, and though she tried to avoid it, Chloe found herself crammed into Jared's back seat between Brandon and Luke. And when they pulled into a Gas-N-Pack on their way out of town, her legs were already cramping. It was going to be a long ride.

While Jared filled the tank, Brandon went inside for a Mountain Dew. Chloe followed him in. "I can't sit like this all the way to the cave," she said. "I feel like one of those Golden Oreos with the chocolate filling."

"It's just to Springfield," Brandon told her. "You and I can ride with Kyle from there."

Luke came through the door and nodded at them. "You getting anything, Chloe?"

"I'm good," she said.

He brushed past them on his way to the coffee. He really was looking fine this morning, Chloe thought. His t-shirt showed off his muscled chest and those jeans

were really hugging his ass. She watched him pour coffee into a foam cup and stir in some powdered creamer.
Yes, he was looking fine indeed.

Brandon nudged her. "You ready?"

She followed him back out to Jared's car. Kassidy
was sitting in the front seat, staring straight ahead, and
Chloe wondered what was going through her brain.
She looked downright depressed and a little pale.
Chloe figured she should feel sorry for her, but for
some reason she couldn't bring herself to take any pity
on her. She was throwing away a perfectly good relationship with a decent guy that was in love with her.
And for what?

Kassidy looked up and stared at something behind
Chloe and Brandon. Chloe turned and saw Luke just
coming out of the convenience store. Kassidy was
watching him. Of course. Why hadn't she seen it before? Kassidy had fallen for Luke. Chloe glanced back
at Luke and saw him and Kassidy make eye contact.
They continued to stare at each other as Luke made his
way toward the car. Chloe's stomach turned. How
long had this been going on?

Jared topped off his tank and latched the fuel door.
"I'm getting some coffee and some snacks," he said.
"Be back in a minute."

Chloe slid into the back seat and Brandon followed.
Luke climbed in on the other side and slammed his
door. "Shitty day," he said.

Chloe caught Kassidy's eyes in the visor mirror.
"Sure is," she said.

The four of them continued to sit in uncomfortable
silence. At the far end of the parking lot a large white-
haired woman in a pink windbreaker was walking a

small black terrier along a strip of grass. They all watched the dog pace back and forth several times before it crouched. Chloe hoped this wasn't going to be the highlight of the day.

The drive to Springfield was drab and uneventful. Kassidy pretended to sleep, but Chloe could see her eyelids flutter in the mirror and watching the passing rain-soaked landscape when she thought no one was looking. Jared and Luke sipped their coffee and Brandon swigged his Mountain Dew. Jared's radio was blaring some kind of death metal crap, so even if anyone had been up for conversation it would have been impossible to hear.

Beside her, Luke drained the rest of his coffee and sat holding the cup. Chloe looked at his hands, at his slender fingers with square nails, and wondered how they would feel on her body. It made her feel panicky and excited at the same time. She let her gaze wander across his jeans and up his dark t-shirt to his red-stubbled chin and caught her breath. He was looking at her and smiling. "Nervous?" he said.

She blinked at him. "What?"

"About the cave. You said the other night you didn't do caves. I'm really surprised you came."

Chloe stared straight ahead and watched the wipers lazily brush across the windshield. "It's no big deal." She could feel him still watching her and her cheeks grew hot.

"If you get scared you can hold my hand," he told her.

From the corner of her eye she saw Brandon shoot a glance at Luke, then turn his attention back to the passing scenery. "I'll be fine," she said. She looked at him and he grinned wider. Against her will, she felt the corners of her own mouth turning upward and she looked away. She wondered again about him and Kassidy and whether more was going than she had previously noticed.

When Chloe was twelve years old, Granny Betty had set her down to, as she said at the time, "have a woman-to-woman talk." Chloe had already been told all about the mechanics of sex and babies by her mother, and she really wasn't looking forward to hearing the same stuff from her grandma. But this had been different. Granny Betty told her all about being a lady, about saving herself because she was smart and how she didn't need to be getting herself mixed up with a do-nothing boy and having babies before she was out of school. She told her to stay on her guard against boys that would try things – sly, nasty things – to get her to spread her legs. "Always remember," Granny told her, "you are being hunted. You are prey. And the devil never sleeps."

Never did those words ring more true than last fall, the week before Thanksgiving. Chloe had left the library after a late shift and was accosted by a man just as she was unlocking her car. He came up behind her, held a knife to her throat and told her he was going to "fuck her good." She managed to get away by stomping on his instep and elbowing him in the stomach, then ran screaming across the quad until she found the campus police patrol unit. It hadn't taken long for them to locate him, still skulking around the parking lot, high on PCP and babbling about witches in the trees. But just because he had been caught didn't mean Chloe could forget it. She still felt the sharp cold blade pressed against her skin, smelled the shit-stench of his breath as his lips grazed her left ear when he whispered, "*I'll fuck you good.*" It was a memory that sometimes still woke her in a cold sweat from a sound sleep, and the reason she kept pepper spray on her at all times.

Chloe looked at Luke now, at his vivid green eyes staring out the car window and wondered if she was seeing the eyes of a different kind of devil. Wondered what kind of nasty thoughts might be going through his mind. Wondered if she were in any of them.

9
LUKE

Luke could feel Chloe's eyes watching him and it sent a thrill through him. And if he weren't so tired from last night he might take the opportunity to move in on her. But today he was totally spent.

He'd left for the Capitol about nine. He'd invited Jared to come along, but of course he was all bummed out about his phone conversation with Kassidy. "Come on, dude," he told him. "You need to get out and have some fun tonight. Kassidy doesn't need to know." But Jared had stayed home. Alone. And Luke had gone on without him. Probably for the best anyway; he didn't need a frowning clown like Jared hanging around him and bringing the party down.

As usual the club was packed. The shitty electro-dance music was pumping and the crowd was gyrating like it was an indoor rave. Which he guessed in a sense it was. Alcohol and drugs flowed freely at the Capitol. Alcohol legally from the bar and drugs anywhere you could get them. He'd only been through the door fifteen minutes before he scored a couple of pre-made joints from a guy next to men's room, and Luke had gone in to smoke one in an empty stall. No one cared what you did in there. At one point he even heard a guy and a girl next to him fucking up a storm. No one else seemed to notice.

When he came out, mellow and red-eyed, he grabbed a beer from the bar and began making his rounds. You never knew who you might see here. Classmates. Ex-girlfriends. The guy who bagged your groceries at Kroger. Once last year he'd even spotted his sociology professor dancing dangerously close with a guy who had to be almost half her age. But tonight there was no one he recognized. Just a bunch of random people dancing and drinking and getting fucked up.

He danced with a few girls until he spotted her, sitting alone at a small table on the sidelines. She was wearing a little red dress of all things, and perched uncomfortably on a tall stool. She had an empty glass in front of her, and her dark eyes indicated she'd either been stood up or abandoned by whoever she'd come with. "What're you drinking?" Luke asked her.

She seemed genuinely surprised by his question, but she smiled at him and tucked her auburn hair behind her ears. "Rum and Coke," she said.

"Would you like another one?" he asked.

"Sure," she said.

He returned from the bar with her drink and another beer for himself and spent the next half hour in deep conversation with her. Her name was Katie, and she had just transferred to Cedar Hill from a small liberal arts college in Nashville. She was a junior, majoring in economics and wondering how she was going to find a decent job in this crappy economy after she graduated. She'd come to the Capitol with her roommate, Carly, and Carly had disappeared into the crowd on the dance floor about two hours ago. "I didn't even want to come here," she told him. "This isn't my kind of music."

"Mine either," he told her. "You want to go someplace else?"

"I'd love to," she said, "but I drove. Carly won't have a way to get back to the dorm."

Luke laughed. "Oh, trust me, she'll get back."

In the end Katie sent Carly a text, then hopped in Luke's truck and rode with him across town to the Wild Horse. It was smaller, quieter, and the jukebox was playing Jason Aldean when they came through the door. Katie seemed to relax at once. They found an empty booth in a corner and proceeded to talk for the next two hours. And when a rambunctious group of drunken cowboys stumbled in a little after one, Luke invited her over to the apartment. And she said yes.

It didn't take much convincing to talk Katie out of her red dress, and before he knew it they were rolling around in his bed and he was fumbling to roll on a condom and she was telling him to hurry up because she wanted him now, goddammit. And then she was on top, riding him like he was a fucking horse and she was crying out and he was exploding and it went on and on. And when she finally slipped off of him and nestled into the crook of his arm, he was left completely overwhelmed, his heart hammering in his chest and his legs tingling with sheer exhaustion. He woke up an hour later, feeling her wet mouth on him, feeling himself stiffen against her tongue as it worked mercilessly on him. He didn't take long; she was very talented. Then he flicked his own tongue across her nipples, feeling them respond, grazing his teeth across them and making her moan. He worked his way down her flat, hard stomach and past her navel, and suddenly he was tasting her, devouring her, and her fingers were tangled in his hair and she was begging him not to stop and then he felt her pulsing against his mouth and she was sighing and melting into the sheets. This morning they awoke at dawn and went at it again, with him on top this time, and she managed to work a finger into his anus. It was the most mind-blowing thing he had ever felt in his life.

And then, as he let her out of his truck by her car on the deserted lot at the Capitol, she smiled at him and said, "I had a good time."

He pulled out his phone. "Can I get your number?"

She continued to smile at him as she opened her door. "Maybe we'll meet up again."

He could only watch as she slipped out and unlocked her car. Was she for real? *Maybe we'll meet up again.* Had she actually said that to him? He left her and drove through the gray drizzle back to the apartment. He was stunned. But he couldn't keep the smile off his face.

The traffic was picking up now as they neared Springfield. A cold fog had settled over the city, and he could barely see the skyline through it. He had brought a hoodie to wear into the cave, but he wished he had it on now. The heat in Jared's piece-of-shit Accord didn't seem to reach back here.

In front of him, Kassidy stirred and stretched.

"Where are we?"

"Almost to Young's," Jared told her. He glanced at her. "You have a good nap?"

Kassidy stared out the window. "Yeah, I did." She locked glances with Luke in the side mirror and looked away.

10

BRANDON

Kyle's black Suburban was parked at the far end of the empty lot, and Brandon could see him sitting behind the wheel with a blue baseball cap pulled down over his eyes. "There he is," he told Jared.

Jared pulled up next to Kyle and the five of them spilled out of the Accord. After forty-five minutes of being cramped up in the back seat, Brandon was ready to stretch and walk around for a bit. He raised a hand in greeting to Kyle.

Kyle climbed out of the SUV. "Hey, man."

"Hey," Brandon said. He introduced the others and Kyle greeted them warmly.

"How far is it to the cave from here?" Jared asked.

"'Bout two hours," Kyle told him. "It's interstate almost the whole way. It's an easy drive."

Kassidy was scouting the surrounding buildings. "Is there any place around here I can use a restroom?"

"Yeah, me, too," Luke said. "That coffee went

straight through me."

"We can go into the store," Kyle said. He dangled a set of keys. "I know the owners, they won't mind."

As they headed across the parking lot, Jared said, "I figure we'll follow you to the cave since I have no idea where I'm going."

Kyle nodded, slipping a key into the side door of the building. "Sure. I'd normally let you guys ride with me, but I've got all that equipment in the back."

"Kassidy and I can just drive separately," Jared said.

Kyle nodded and swung open the door to a dark hallway. He flipped a switch and lights blazed on inside an administrative area. "To your left."

As the others headed toward the restrooms, Brandon stood at the doorway with Kyle. "Appreciate all this," he said.

Kyle looked at him. "What? Letting you pee?"

Brandon laughed. "Taking us out there. Providing all the equipment."

"No problem, man."

Brandon looked down at the scuffed toes of his Skechers. "How was your date last night?"

Kyle shrugged. "It was all right. She's a family friend. A little older than me. She's got a twelve-year-old kid."

"Think you'll see her again?"

"Hard to say. We got along okay. The kid thing scares me, though, you know? I mean, I want kids someday, but. . . Jesus, a twelve-year-old? I'm just not sure I'm ready for that."

Brandon nodded. Guiltily, he felt a small sense of relief that Kyle didn't seem too interested in this girl. Even if he knew there would be nothing but friendship between Kyle and himself, he still wasn't ready to share him with someone else. Especially a woman, who could give him what Brandon couldn't. And as long as Kyle remained single, there was at least a tiny fraction of hope. Right?

A few minutes later, with Brandon riding shotgun, Luke and Chloe in the backseat of the Suburban, and Jared and Kassidy following along behind them, Kyle rolled out of the lot and headed up the ramp to the interstate. He glanced at Luke and Chloe in the rearview mirror and grinned. "Don't you two be messing around on my leather seats back there."

Brandon caught Chloe's eye and saw her face flush. "We'll be good," she said. Brandon smiled at her, and she gave him an angry look.

Luke asked about the Suburban, and he and Kyle chatted happily away for the next thirty minutes about horsepower and torque and four-wheel-drive, and Brandon found himself wishing he knew at least a little bit about engines so he could throw in an intelligent comment here and there. Kyle seemed to know a lot about a lot of things. He was smart and decent, and his time in the army had given him an appreciation for life. It just didn't seem fair. Why did the perfect man have to come into Brandon's life at this moment and turn out to be straight?

Brandon looked back at Chloe again. Her eyes were wide and blank as Luke droned on beside her. She caught Brandon looking at her and made a slashing motion across her throat. It was their secret sign for "Kill me now." Brandon snorted and covered it with a cough. It was going to be a long drive.

II
JARED

They had been driving without talking now for forty-five minutes, following Kyle's black SUV and listening to the Slipknot CD. It had started to repeat.

At first Jared thought Kassidy was sleeping, but he glanced at her and saw that she was staring blankly out the window. The wipers made a sweep across the windshield and fell still. She blinked and continued to stare.

He reached over and turned down the music. "So," he said, "you want to tell me what's going on?"

She looked at him. "What do you mean?"

"I mean, what's wrong with you? You're not yourself. For the past couple of weeks you've just been, I don't know. . . preoccupied."

She took a deep breath and turned her gaze back to the cedar forest rushing by. "I've just been thinking. . . "

He waited for a moment, and when she didn't answer he said, "About what?"

Beside him he saw a tear glistening on her cheek. "I just wonder if it's over."

The wipers swept again.

A sick knot formed in his belly. "If what's over? You mean *us*?"

She nodded and wiped her face with the heel of her hand. Another tear slipped out of the corner of her eye and this time it rolled down and dripped off her chin. "I've been thinking about it for a long time."

"How long?"

She sniffed. "About six months now."

He jerked the steering wheel. "Six months? You've been wanting to break up with me for six *months*?"

"Yes," she whispered. Then shook her head. "No. Not entirely."

He glanced at her. "What the fuck, Kassidy? What the *fuck*?"

She was crying openly now. "I don't know. It's complicated."

He pounded his fist on the steering wheel. "It's complicated." He blew out a breath. "This isn't some goddamn Facebook update, you know."

She turned away from him, staring out at the gray landscape. "This isn't easy."

"Damn right it's not." He focused on the taillights of Kyle's Suburban. "When were you going to tell me?"

"Tonight."

He shook his head, letting that sink in. "Why did you even come today?"

"I don't know."

He gripped the wheel tighter. "Is there somebody

else?"

"No."

He glanced at her. "You're sure?"

She looked back at him with red-brimmed eyes. "I said no. There's nobody else."

He turned his gaze back to the wet roadway. The wipers swept across the windshield again. Beside him, Kassidy was sniffling and wiping her eyes on the sleeve of her jersey. After a moment he reached down and turned up the music.

12
CHLOE

Luke and Kyle's conversation about trucks and motors had finally petered out. Now Kyle had started in about his ten years in the army and how the government didn't seem to care about the veterans it was disgorging back into civilian life. Even Luke's eyes were glazing over.

So when she sensed a lull in Kyle's diatribe, she said, "So what's the story about this place being haunted?"

Kyle glanced back at her. "Old Indian tale," he said. "The Algonquins, I think. Said the cave was inhabited by some kind of spirit. A bad spirit. Something that ate people."

Luke looked up in alarm. "*Ate* people?" He caught Chloe's gaze and she knew he was thinking of the cavers who had disappeared.

"Sounds like a wendigo," Chloe said. "Native American mythology is full of spirits, both good and bad. But a wendigo is a little different. A wendigo was once human but became a monster after resorting to cannibalism. The legend says a wendigo is doomed to roam the earth forever, always hungering for human flesh."

Brandon shifted uncomfortably. "So those cavers that disappeared. . . "

"I doubt they were eaten by a wendigo," Chloe said. "It's just a myth."

"How do you know all this stuff?" Kyle said.

"She's a sociology major," Luke said.

"Anthropology minor," Chloe added.

"So what do you think happened to those guys?" Luke asked Kyle.

Kyle shrugged. "I figure they just got lost. Got into some part of the cave no one had been in before. Got in trouble somewhere. Maybe got stuck. It's easy to do if you don't know what you're doing."

"So this wendigo," Brandon said, "what does it look like?"

"I saw a drawing once," Chloe said. "It was tall, kind of looked like a werewolf. But that's assuming you can see it all. It's a shape-shifter. It can look like anything."

Luke looked back at her. "Even people?"

"I suppose. But mostly animals – wolves, bears, birds. . . things the Native Americans would have been familiar with."

"Well," Kyle said, "let's hope all we see are a couple of bats."

Chloe sat up. "Bats?" Oh, God, she hated bats.

"Yep. Bound to be some in there."

Chloe blew out a breath and sank back into the seat. Great.

13
KASSIDY

Kassidy was glad when Jared turned up the CD. She had no desire for him to hear her crying, and she was sure he didn't want to listen. Insanely, she wondered what he would say if she chose this moment to tell him about her and Luke. But that wasn't going to happen. She would carry that to her grave, and as long as Luke and Jared were sharing an apartment she was confident Luke would keep his mouth shut, too.

She knew coming along today was stupid. She should have just stayed home. She had studying to do, although how much she could get done while brooding over Jared, she didn't know.

She had caught Luke watching her a couple of times this morning. And his expression was one of sadness. Pity, almost, and it made her angry. What right did he have to pity her? Did he think she was pining away for him? Did he think she was losing sleep over him?

But I am.

Her mind kept racing back to that night in Luke's bed, feeling his large hands – so much smoother and nimble than Jared's – playing over her body. The long, slow movements of his hips, not Jared's rushed, desperate thrusts. Luke's solid arms wrapped around her when they were done. Luke's soft, thick lips grazing the back of her neck.

Kassidy closed her eyes and the tears squeezed down her cheeks. She didn't seem to have the strength to wipe them away.

14
LUKE

Kyle pulled into a QuikStop after they'd been driving an hour and a half. Jared and Kassidy eased into the space beside them. "Last chance for a bathroom, boys and girls," Kyle said. "And if you want any snacks, get them now."

Earlier they had passed an ancient faded billboard for the cave promising underground boat tours and an exotic petting zoo. "Think we'll see any animals?" Luke joked.

"Nothing you'd want to pet," Kyle told him.

"How much farther?" Jared said.

"'Bout ten miles," Kyle said.

As the others drifted toward the store, Luke caught sight of Kassidy and fell in behind her. "So how's it going?"

"Fine," she said, not looking at him.

"You don't sound fine." He put a hand on her shoulder and she spun around. Her eyes were red and puffy. "Is everything okay with you and Jared?"

She shook her head and turned back toward the store.

Behind him, he heard Jared say, "Hey."

Luke turned to him. "What's up with Kassidy?"

Jared shrugged. "I think she wants to break up."

Luke blew out a breath. "No shit?"

"Yeah."

"That sucks, man."

Jared nodded. "Tell me about it." He brushed past and headed for the door of the QuikStop.

So Kassidy was getting ready to dump Jared. Took her long enough. And no wonder she'd been moping around the past few days and giving Luke those longing glances. It all made sense now. But if she thought they could pick up where they left off that night in bed, she had a big surprise coming. Luke wasn't ready to be tied down by anyone, especially Kassidy. Although, he thought with a smile, he still wouldn't mind an interlude with Chloe.

Chloe was standing at the check-out line now, just in front of Brandon. She was holding a couple of bottled waters and a bag of trail mix. She caught him staring at her and smiled – just barely, but enough that he could see before she turned her flushed face away.

Yeah, there was a possibility there. Maybe he just needed to keep plugging away. She would eventually come around.

15
BRANDON

Back outside, Jared opened his trunk and they all slipped their purchases into their backpacks. There was a thick tension between Jared and Kassidy. Kassidy looked as though she'd been crying, and Brandon wondered if they'd had a fight.

Chloe came up beside her and her words were just barely audible: "You want to ride with Kyle? I don't care to ride with Jared the rest of the way."

Kassidy shook her head. "It's fine. We're almost there."

Back in Kyle's Suburban, Brandon leaned back toward Chloe. "What was that all about?"

Chloe shook her head. "Nothing."

Brandon felt a stab of irritation. It wasn't like Chloe to keep secrets from him.

Kyle slammed his door and cranked the engine. "All set? Next stop, Devil's Catacombs."

Just past the QuikStop, the landscape changed to

dense pine forest. The woods looked dark and deep, shrouded in a fog that had taken over since the rain let up. A sign pointed the way toward Indian Chief Cave, and Brandon found himself wishing they were going there instead. Not that Chloe's story about the wendigo had unnerved him, but something about exploring caverns where people might have been lost forever bothered him. He was thankful Kyle was with them.

He watched Kyle's strong fingers grip the steering wheel and wondered how different things might have been had it just been the two of them today. Kyle had really opened up on that hiking trip to the lake. Maybe it would have been Brandon's turn to open up, to let Kyle know his true feelings for him. Maybe Kyle was hiding some secret feelings as well.

And maybe Kyle would have beaten the shit out of him.

Brandon had never known what to do about expressing his interest to another guy. There were times when he thought sure the other person felt the same way, but something inside refused to let Brandon explore it any further. He felt trapped between what he really wanted and what he had been told all his life was an abomination to God. And to his mother. So he had learned over the years to push those feelings aside, to ignore them, to pretend they didn't exist. But it was becoming more difficult. Especially now that he was in college and there were so many unabashedly gay students around – people who had no qualms or preconceived condemnations about their orientation. He longed to be like those folks, to be free and uninhibited and happy. But he knew the possibility was slim. At least for now.

The Suburban pulled off the main road onto a

cracked, weed-choked two-lane. A peeling wooden sign proclaimed "OPEN YEAR-ROUND." A faded red arrow pointed down the road that sloped into the dense woods. "This is it," Kyle said, heading down the hill.

The forest encroached from both sides, and nothing could be seen beyond the trees right next to them. It was as if the pines along the road were a screen for a black void beyond. A vacuum where the sun never penetrated. The air seemed chillier and Kyle's windshield began to fog over. Brandon shivered. "Did it just get colder in here?"

The SUV lurched to a stop. Ahead of them two concrete barriers stretched across the roadway, riddled with colorful graffiti and surrounded with broken bottles and rusting beer cans.

"What's this?" Luke said.

Kyle put the truck in park and killed the engine. "This is it. The end of the line. We walk from here."

16
JARED

Jared popped open the trunk and began unloading the backpacks. He and Kassidy had not spoken since leaving the QuikStop. When he hauled out her backpack, she took it from him silently without meeting his eyes. So now she wasn't even looking at him anymore.

Kyle and Brandon were unloading equipment from the back of the Suburban and laying it out along the cracked pavement. Helmets with lights, knee pads, elbow pads and safety belts with thick nylon ropes. Kyle seemed like an all right guy, though Jared had barely said two words to him. He looked confident and strong, no doubt from his time in the army, and he set out the supplies with military precision.

"After you guys get your jackets and packs on, we'll get suited up with the safety equipment," Kyle said. "I brought along some extra flashlights, and I want you each to take one. Just in case something happens to your headlamp."

"Like what?" Kassidy asked, her tone tinged with alarm. Her hand was struggling to find the sleeve of her hoodie. Any other time Jared would have helped her into it.

"Anything," Kyle said. "The battery could go out. You could knock against something and break it. You always need a backup."

In spite of the chilly air, by the time Jared was strapped into his equipment, he could feel a trickle of sweat running down the back of his neck. None of the items were heavy, but the knee and elbow pads were awkward and reminded him of the six weeks he'd spent in a cast. His flannel shirt moved uncomfortably underneath the backpack, almost binding his back and shoulders, and the yellow helmet was tight as a drum around his head.

"Let's head down there," Kyle said, climbing over the concrete barrier.

Except for the drizzle dripping from the pines, the forest on either side of them was eerily quiet. No birds. No scurrying of wildlife in the undergrowth. Nothing. Grass and weeds browned by the autumn sprouted through the crumbled pavement which was littered with beer cans and other debris. "You ever party out here, man?" Jared said to Kyle.

Kyle shook his head. "Not me. Looks like somebody does, though."

"Looks like some of the places I used to hang out back in high school," Luke said.

"Where you from?" Kyle asked.

"Vicksburg, Mississippi. We always had us a party going on come the weekend."

"Yeah, until your dad caught wind of it and practically put the whole school on lockdown," Jared said.

Kyle gave them a puzzled look and Luke blew out a breath. "My dad was the principal of my high school."

Kyle grimaced. "Oh, that must have sucked."

"You don't know the half of it."

They followed the slope down a twisting lane. If possible, the forest turned even darker. The drizzle that had plagued them all the way from Springfield seemed to have quit for the moment, but the clouds were thicker and looked heavy with rain.

Behind him, Chloe and Kassidy were bringing up the rear. Kassidy stopped occasionally to snap a photo with her phone, of what he couldn't imagine. There was nothing but pine trees and crumbling blacktop.

"So," Jared said, catching back up to Kyle, "how many times have you been here?"

Kyle looked at him, then back at the others. "Okay, I'll be honest. I've only been here once. When I was a kid."

Jared stopped walking and let that sink in for a moment. "Wait. When you were a kid? So you haven't been here since. . . "

"Since the place closed twenty years ago," Kyle finished for him.

"But you said you'd been here lots of times," Brandon said.

"No, I said I'd been *caving* lots of times."

"So you got no idea what this place is like inside?" Luke said.

Kyle shrugged. "I've seen pictures. Talked to some people on an online messageboard. One guy drew me a map."

Kassidy was shaking her head. "This is bullshit."

"Really, it's no big deal," Kyle said, holding up his hands. "We just stick to the main cave area, maybe walk down and see the underground river. We won't go anywhere else. No tight places, no crawling around, nothing like that."

"You promise?" Chloe said, her eyes narrowed.

"I swear," Kyle said.

Kassidy lowered her head and rubbed her temples. "God, I knew I should have stayed home."

"Everyone just relax," Kyle said. "We'll be fine, I promise."

17
CHLOE

As the others started back down the hill, Chloe grabbed the tail of Brandon's sweatshirt. "Did you know about this?" she said through clenched teeth, but she could tell by the expression on his face that he didn't.

"I had no idea," Brandon said.

"Well this doesn't make me feel too safe," Chloe whispered.

"It'll be alright," Brandon said. "Don't panic."

She watched him follow the others and realized that's exactly what she was doing. She was panicking.

Calm down.

She took a deep breath and started down the slope. Just behind Kyle and Jared she could see Luke, and she wished she was walking with him, that he was holding her hand and telling her it would be okay, that they would just take a quick trip inside the cave and right back out. He had promised the other night he would

protect her. And she wondered now if he was completely joking or if he'd been half-serious.

"I see the entrance," Kyle shouted back at them.
"We're here."

Around the bend was a weed-infested parking lot
surrounded by several squat, run-down buildings. A
large paneled sign on the roof of the largest one proclaimed "DEVIL'S CATACOMBS" and below that,
"NATURE'S WONDERLAND." Other signs pointed
the way to the petting zoo and a coffee shop.

"Now," Kyle said, "the way I remember it, the entrance was through the gift shop, that main building
there." He pointed toward the sprawling clapboard
structure in front of them adorned with a sign that said
"Enter here for tours!" He headed toward it, motioning
the others to follow.

The doors to the shop hung awkwardly, their locks
and windows having been broken long ago. Kyle
swung open one of the metal framed doors with a rusty
creak. "Lights on, everyone," he said. "Looks like
there's broken glass everywhere, so be careful. Number one rule is, stay together. Nobody wanders off on
their own."

Chloe inched closer to Brandon and followed the
others through the door into the darkened shop. She
reached up and switched on her headlamp. Dust-coated
overturned shelves and moldy boxes littered the floor.
More graffiti covered the walls and ceiling. On the
"Entrance" sign that hung crookedly over a turnstile,
someone had spray painted "to Hell."

Brandon looked at her. "You don't have to go in,
you know. You could wait out here."

Chloe shook her head. She was tired of always

hanging back, of regretting missed opportunities and experiences. "I'll go if you will," she said, and Brandon smiled at her.

She noticed Kassidy was holding Jared's hand. What was going on there? Had Kassidy had a change of heart, or was she just nervous?

"Over here," Kyle said, leaning against the turnstile. He had pulled out a crumpled sheet of paper and was studying it in the glow from his headlamp. He motioned to the steel doors behind him. "Once we go in there, there's a concrete ramp that takes us down about fifty yards to the cavern, then we're actually in the cave." He looked at Luke. "Want to help me with this?"

The rusty bulkhead door opened with a grating screech of protest, with Luke and Kyle grunting with the strain, and a blast of cold stale air rushed out at them.

"Let's go," Kyle said.

18

KASSIDY

Kassidy squeezed Jared's hand tighter, grateful to be with him.

He looked down at her. "You want to stay up here? Maybe you and Chloe could wait for us."

"I'll be all right." She glanced at him. He was staring at her, his blue eyes intense and searching, and she felt hurt welling up inside her again. She had to look away before she started crying.

They were in a man-made tunnel of concrete walls molded to resemble rock, dotted here and there with graffiti. The floor sloped gently downward, and they inched their way forward. The lights from their helmets rippled over the ceiling, giving an almost strobe effect, and Kassidy felt her head swim. The air, cool and dry, was completely odorless.

"Watch your step," Kyle called from up ahead. "There's some water here. Floor may be slick."

Chloe gave a startled cry. "Luke, get your hand off

my ass."

"My bad," Luke said. "But how'd you know it was me?"

"Well, it wasn't Brandon, he's in front of me."

"Hey, keep it in your pants, man," Jared said. He glanced at Kassidy and shook his head.

She squeezed his hand again and leaned toward his warmth. Even though she was wearing the hoodie, she was freezing. "It's cold in here," she whispered to Jared.

"Yeah, they say Indian Chief Cave stays around fifty-five degrees," Jared said. "I would assume it's the same here."

Ahead of them, the others came to a halt. "What's going on?" Kassidy said. She peered around Luke and Chloe.

"End of the tunnel," Kyle said.

The others shifted, and Kassidy could see two gray metal doors in the shifting light. They had been chained shut. A large sign posted on one of them proclaimed "DANGER – KEEP OUT." Below it, someone had spray-painted, "FUCK YOU."

"Well, this sucks," Luke said. "What do we do now?"

"No worries," Kyle said. "They said on the messageboard we might have to take an alternate route."

"I don't like the sound of that," Chloe said.

"Let's get back up top," Kyle said. "We'll regroup."

"I've got some bolt cutters in my truck," Luke said as they moved back up the ramp. "If I'd known, I could've brought them."

"There's another way in," Kyle said. "We just have to find it."

They emerged into the lifeless daylight and gathered in front of the gift shop. Now that they were outside, Kassidy let go of Jared's hand and stood awkwardly next to him. It seemed silly now, grabbing him like that in the dark. He probably thought she was a fool.

"So what's the plan?" Brandon said, switching off his lamp.

Kyle motioned beyond the dilapidated buildings on the far side of the parking lot. "There's another entrance down there, where the river exits the cave, close to where the boat tours used to dock."

"River?" Chloe said. "Will we have to get in the water?"

Kyle shook his head. "It's a hidden entrance in the rock. Messageboard says it's kinda hard to find. But it goes directly into the cave." He stroked his beard and gave them an apologetic smile. "We may have to do a little crawling."

"Oh, *hell* no," Chloe said. "You said there wouldn't be any of that."

"Yeah, I'm not doing that either," Kassidy said. She thought of what Jared had said, about her and Chloe waiting for the guys up here. "You all can go ahead."

Jared put an arm around her. "At least come look at it with us. It might not be as bad as you think."

"I think it's only about a fifty-foot crawl," Kyle said. "Not very strenuous."

Kassidy locked glances with Chloe. Chloe looked as though she had been slapped. "I guess we can see what it looks like," Kassidy said.

"I'm not making any promises," Chloe said, "but I guess it won't hurt to look."

Luke took her hand. "I won't let anything happen to

you. I promise."

Chloe looked at him, but she didn't make any effort to pull her hand back. "I'm counting on you."

Beside her, Brandon watched the exchange with an expression of fascination. Kassidy expected him to make some kind of snarky comment, but he was silent. He looked amused that Chloe was allowing Luke to move in on her. She wondered again what was going through Chloe's head and what the story was between her and Brandon.

Her thoughts were interrupted by Jared's fingers as they mindlessly played with the end of her ponytail. She never should have taken his hand earlier, never should have touched him. Never should have met that longing gaze in his eyes.

She tilted her head and rested it against his shoulder.

19

LUKE

Chloe was letting him hold her hand. She had even intertwined her fingers with his. He felt a rush and a sudden throbbing in his groin. He had finally worn her down. He glanced at her, but she wasn't looking at him. He followed her gaze and saw that she was staring at Brandon's back.

Poor old Brandon. Luke felt he ought to feel some kind of guilt, edging Brandon out that way, but hell, he hadn't made a move on Chloe in two years that he knew of. And evidently Chloe had decided enough was enough. He watched Brandon plod along in front of them, and he wondered if maybe Brandon had *never* had any intentions of being with Chloe. Maybe he'd just wanted to be friends with her all along. Maybe he wasn't into girls. Maybe –

"What's that?" Kassidy said behind them. She was pointing at a small fenced in area off to their right. Gates and chicken wire stretched across rotting timbers, grown up with weeds and vines.

"Must be part of the old petting zoo," Jared said.

"No, *that*," she said, stabbing her finger in the air. "Next to the fence."

Then Luke saw it, too. A patch of dark fur and blood lying in the tall brown grass in one of the abandoned pens. He moved closer.

It was an animal of some kind. Maybe a deer. He could make out hooves on the ends of spindly legs and a smallish head with large ears. But the fur was the wrong color. It was dark, almost black. Its body had been ripped open, and the ground around it was dark with blood.   The skin was ragged with what looked like claw marks. White ribs poked through red flesh and surrounded the dark empty cavity where intestines should have been.

Beside him, Chloe covered her mouth. "That's not a deer. Is it?"

Kyle shook his head. "Doesn't look like it."

Chloe continued to stare. "What *is* that?"

"It's a fresh kill," Brandon said, "whatever it is."

"What did it?" Kassidy said. Her eyes were wide, and she looked as though she might cry.

"Maybe a bobcat," Kyle said. "Probably some around here."

"We must have scared it off," Jared said.

"Be careful, everyone," Kyle said. "It may still be close by. If it's still hungry, it'll be back."

"Okay, I don't like this at all," Chloe said.

Luke squeezed her hand. "It'll be all right," he said. But he had to admit, the thought of some wild animal lurking around and maybe watching them didn't make him feel very safe. "Just stick with me."

They followed Kyle down the path, past rickety, peeling signs pointing the way to the boat tours. Wooden benches, rotted by neglect and broken by vandals lined the weed-choked trail through the pines.

"Maybe we should go back," Kassidy said.

"We'll be all right," Jared told her.

"But what if that thing comes back?"

"If it's a bobcat, it probably won't bother us now," Kyle said. "They're afraid of people and we're away from its kill."

"What if it's not a bobcat?" Chloe said.

Brandon shot her a look. "What else could it be?"

"I don't know," she said. "A bear. A mountain lion."

"Nothing like that around here," Kyle said. "Let's just keep moving. I think we're almost there."

Just below them the green sluggish water came into view. The remnants of an old dock floated along the bank, just up from where the river emerged from a dark cavern. Only one boat remained, half-sunk in the opaque water. A small ticket booth slanted at an impossible angle, its windows shattered and its wooden façade peeling and rotten. The air was deathly silent.

"Looks like we're first in line," Luke said.

Kassidy pointed toward the yawning cave. "We're not going in that way, are we?"

"Nope," Kyle said. He pointed at the bluff off to the right. "The opening's supposed to be over there somewhere. We'll have to look for it." He and Brandon headed off away from the rest of them.

Chloe surveyed the knee-high weeds covering the small slope. "Great. We'll probably get covered in ticks."

Luke put his hand on her waist. "I'll help you pull them off," he said. He winked at her and she elbowed him in the ribs.

Behind them, Kassidy held Jared's hands clasped to her chest. "Jared, I don't like this, I really don't. I want to go back."

"But we're almost inside," Jared said. "It'll be all right, baby."

"I just want to go back and wait in the car. I don't want to go in there. I don't want to be here."

"Kassidy," Jared said, his voice sharp, "calm down. Don't freak out on me. It's all right. I don't want you sitting out there all by yourself."

"But Chloe will come with me." She looked at Chloe with pleading, tear-filled eyes. "You'll come with me, won't you?"

Chloe sighed. "Girl, if there's some kind of wild animal out there, I think we're better off all staying together."

"Then let's all go back," Kassidy said. "Please. Let's just go back to the car and forget about this."

"I think we found it," Brandon called. Kyle and Brandon had reached a shadowy outcropping. Kyle was squatted on the ground and Brandon was stooped over him.

"That was easy," Jared said. He looked back at Kassidy. "See? It's a piece of cake. We'll go in, we'll come right back out."

Chloe unhooked her hand from Luke's and put her arm around Kassidy. "Stay with me," she told her. "It won't be so bad."

Kassidy looked at her. "I thought you were scared, too."

"I'm terrified," Chloe said. "But I'm a lot more scared of staying out here where some wild animal might eat me." The two of them hugged up together and moved up the slope toward Brandon and Kyle.

Luke shot a glance at Jared and shrugged.

Jared shook his head. "What the fuck ever, man."

20

BRANDON

Brandon watched as Kyle flipped on his lamp and peered into the opening. It was about waist high, but wide. The smooth walls curved into the darkness beyond, past the reach of Kyle's light.

Brandon thought of the animal carcass they'd seen at the petting zoo. "You don't think anything's living in there, do you?"

"Don't see any tracks around here," Kyle said. "And it's a little muddy out here, so if something had been here in the past day or so we'd know it."

The others had gathered around them, stooping and craning their necks to see into the tunnel.

"See anything?" Luke said.

"Just a cave," Kyle said. "Floor looks dry in there. It's big and roomy. Shouldn't be a hard crawl." He looked back at them. "I'm going in. You guys follow me. Brandon, you take up the rear."

Brandon watched the others switch on their headlamps and follow Kyle into the opening. Chloe trailed behind Luke, and Kassidy was right behind. Kassidy's face was tear-streaked and her eyes red-rimmed. She looked nearly hysterical. He wondered if her going in was a good idea, but there didn't seem to be much of a choice at this point. No one else was turning back, and it didn't seem safe for her to stay out alone.

Jared grabbed Brandon's arm. "Help me watch Kassidy, okay?"

Brandon nodded. "She looks pretty rough."

"Yeah." Jared ducked and slid into the tunnel.

Brandon took one last look around at the abandoned boat dock, then followed Jared into the darkness. The dirt floor was cool and dry against his palms, and the sounds of shuffling and occasional grunts were stifled and flat. He could see nothing but the smooth limestone walls lined by eons of weathering and the soles of Jared's sneakers moving in front of his face.

"Everybody okay back there?" Kyle called.

"You okay, baby?" Jared said to Kassidy, and she gave a small whimper.

"I think we're all right," Brandon said.

"I do not like this," Chloe called out. "I do not like this, Sam-I-Am."

"We're almost there," Kyle said. "I can see the end of the tunnel."

Brandon followed Jared's shoes through the darkness, watching his hands plod through the dust and dirt. Sweat had begun to trickle from underneath his helmet. A drop slid down his nose and landed on his knuckles. He hadn't expected to get so hot after the coolness of the tunnel behind the gift shop. He supposed it must be all their body heat concentrated into such a small area.

All that exertion and exhaling.

The passage suddenly ended, and Brandon realized he had emerged into a much larger space. He got to his feet and looked around him.

They were about a hundred yards away from where the river made its way past them from the vast blackness and exited the cave. Dim light from the opening filtered down to where they all stood blinking in the glare of the headlamps, looking at each other.

Jared had his arms wrapped around Kassidy's waist. "You okay?"

She nodded, and her helmet wobbled on her head. "It was better than I thought. This isn't so bad."

"See? I told you it would be all right."

Luke took Chloe's hand. "Everything okay?"

She was breathing heavily. She had edged over next to Luke. "I guess so." She bent over and rested her elbows on her knees. "I'm not claustrophobic, but *damn* that was tight." She looked up at Kyle. "Your idea of 'big and roomy' is a lot different from mine."

"I've been through a lot tighter than that, believe me," Kyle said. He unfolded his map and held it in front of his eyes.

"What now?" Jared asked.

Kyle nodded his head behind him, toward the pitch blackness beyond the last vestiges of daylight. "That way. There should be a passage that intersects with the main cave." He folded the map and slipped it into his pocket. "Let's go." Kyle climbed up a small abutment that jutted out from the cave wall. He turned and held out a hand to Luke. "You help the girls up," he told him.

Luke pulled up Kassidy, then Chloe. He held out his

hand to Jared and grinned. "Help you, miss?"

Jared glared at him. "Fuck you." He scrambled over the rock and looked back at Brandon. "Come on, it's not so bad."

Brandon looked at the outcropping just above waist height. He wondered whether he could maneuver his bulk that high without pulling something. Or ripping his jeans. He pulled off his backpack and slung it up next to Jared's feet, then wiped the sweat off his face with the sleeve of his shirt and planted his hands on the cool stone. His feet flailed for a hold, and he finally pushed himself upward with the toe of his shoe. His hips cleared the edge of the rock and he rolled over on-to the surface like a beached whale. "I've got to go on a diet," he said.

"This way," Kyle said, disappearing into an opening in the cave wall.

Brandon shouldered his pack and followed the oth-ers into the narrow passage. White arrows spray-painted on the rock showed the way. His sides weren't exactly touching the walls, but it was a tighter squeeze than the tunnel they had crawled through. "How far is it?" he called out to Kyle.

Kyle's voice came back muffled and unintelligible. "What?"

Jared turned and said, "He says he's not sure."

Great. Behind him, the passageway disappeared as the inky darkness swallowed it up. Ahead of him, he concentrated on Jared's blue hoodie and green back-pack, on the others' headlamps dancing across the rocky surface of the passage, endless walls of lifeless gray limestone punctuated at intervals with white ar-rows.

"Pretty narrow here, buddy," Jared said.

Brandon watched him slide through the opening, his chest and backpack scraping the rock on either side.

Brandon stopped. "I don't think I can get through there," he said, feeling slight panic in the pit of his belly.

"Sure you can," Jared told him. "Take off your pack and hand it to me."

Brandon shrugged out of the backpack and slipped it to Jared. "I'm telling you I can't get through there. I'm too fat."

"You can make it," Jared said. "Kyle made it through and he's as big as you are. Think skinny thoughts, dude."

Brandon turned sideways and slid between the walls. For one horrible moment, he was sure he would get stuck. Rock pressed against him from both sides. He could feel his heart pounding.

"Come on, Brandon," Jared said. "Exhale."

Brandon blew out all the breath in his lungs and felt himself slipping through. He staggered out on the other side. His heart still hammered in his chest and sweat dripped from his face.

Jared handed over his backpack. "You okay, buddy?"

"I'm fine," Brandon said. The last thing he needed was for Jared to take pity on him, like he was weak and completely incompetent. "Let's go."

The passageway opened up a bit, but the floor seemed rockier and looser. Brandon struggled to maintain his balance, grasping the walls and pulling himself along.

Jared glanced back at him. "Kyle says to be careful,

there's a lot of loose rock."

"No shit," Brandon said.

He inched along behind Jared, grateful for the company but hoping Jared wasn't hanging back just for him. Jared had always intimidated him for some reason. Whether it was his good looks or his confident personality, he wasn't sure. But Brandon always felt like a bumbling fool around him, like he constantly had to prove himself. Just like Friday night when he'd realized he was completely out of cash to pay for the pizza. Jared had always been kind to him, and he'd never said anything disparaging about Brandon's weight. Or anything else for that matter. Jared was a good guy.

Luke wouldn't have waited for him. Luke was too busy sniffing around Chloe like a dog in heat. Brandon had been watching the two of them all day, noticing how Luke took any opportunity he could to touch her, to engage her in conversation. He was all horned up, and everyone could see it.

He had to admit feeling a spark of jealousy when Chloe let Luke hold her hand. She'd always said Luke made her nervous, that she knew all he wanted was sex. And Brandon was pretty sure she was still a virgin. Something must have changed if she was allowing Luke that close. Maybe she was loosening up. Maybe she was ready to shed her shy librarian image and open herself up to new things. New people. New possibilities. Or maybe she was just scared and wanted to hold somebody's hand. He would have to ask her about it later.

A sudden cry from Jared broke him from his thoughts.

"What's wrong?"

Jared was grimacing and clutching his leg. "I twisted my fucking knee," he said through clenched teeth. "My bad one."

"Hold up!" Brandon called out. "Jared's hurt!"

The others appeared out of the darkness at once. "What happened?" Kassidy said.

"Caught my foot in those loose rocks," Jared said, his face contorted in agony. "I tried to pull it loose. . . "

Kassidy put her arms around his shoulders. "It's okay, babe. Just relax." She turned back to Kyle. "We've got to get him someplace where he can stretch out."

"Let's keep going," Kyle said. "It shouldn't be much farther."

"Can you make it?" Brandon said.

"I think so," Jared breathed. He wriggled out of his backpack and handed it to Brandon. "Here, take this."

"Sure."

Kyle looked around at the walls of the passage. "This part is different," he said. "This is sandstone. Not very stable from the looks of it."

"Well, let's get out of here, then," Luke said.

"Once we make it to the main cave, we'll be okay," Kyle said. "We've got to be close. The messageboard says – "

"You sure put a lot of stock in that messageboard," Luke said. "Did anybody on the messageboard tell you we'd be in an unstable passageway?"

"Not really."

"What do you mean, 'not really'?" Luke's eyes were narrow and piercing.

Kyle swallowed and looked around at them. "Somebody said it could be dangerous through here. I didn't tell you guys because I figured you wouldn't come in."

"Fucking right we wouldn't have come in," Luke spat. "What the hell's wrong with you?"

"Guys!" Jared called out. "Stop it. Let's just get away from this area so I can stretch my leg out. I think I'll be all right once I can rest it for a bit. We might as well push on through."

"He's right," Chloe said. "We've already come this far."

Luke and Kyle glared at each other for a moment, then Kyle turned and headed off into the darkness ahead. "Let's get a move-on."

The others followed. Jared limped along, leaning on Kassidy's shoulders in front of him.

"You okay, Kassidy?" Brandon called.

"I'm fine," she said, but her voice sounded weak.

The loose sandstone rock finally gave way to smooth limestone, and the floor of the passage leveled out. And suddenly the narrow walls disappeared as they emerged into a black void. There was nothing except the small pool of light given off by their headlamps.

"I think we're here," Kyle said.

21

CHLOE

Chloe grabbed onto Luke's hand and strained to see into the darkness. She could see no cave walls, no cave ceiling. She couldn't hear anything except the sound of her own heartbeat in her ears. It was like standing in the middle of nothing.

A hiss interrupted the silence, and she saw that Kyle had ignited a flare. He pitched it off into the dark and a steady, pulsating blue-white glow filled the cavern.

The ceiling of the cave looked to be a good hundred feet up, and the gray walls stretched into infinity on either side. Stalagmites grew up from the floor, rounded like melted candles. Farther down, columns carved by water over millions of years lined the passage. As dramatic as it was, Chloe couldn't help but feel a little underwhelmed. It took her a moment, but she finally realized what was lacking was *color*. Everything was gray. Lifeless. Dull.

Just as she was turning back toward the others,

something at the far edge of the light caught her eye. Something appeared to be moving. She squinted and it disappeared. She watched for a few seconds but saw nothing else. It must have been a trick of the light from the flare. Or she was just seeing things. She was still a little freaked out by the dead animal they had seen. That and the talk of a bobcat roaming around.

Brandon and Kassidy helped Jared to the floor. He stretched his leg out and unstrapped the kneepad, then began massaging his leg.

"Better?" Kassidy asked.

Jared nodded. He looked up at Brandon. "Get me a water out of my pack."

Luke was suddenly in Kyle's face. "I oughta beat the living shit out of you, man. You don't know anything about this place, do you? Just what you got off the internet."

Kyle's face was hard. "Back off, dude."

"You could've got us killed."

"No one's killed," Jared said.

"No, but you're hurt pretty bad."

"I'll be all right. This happens to me all the time."

Luke paced back and forth like a bantam rooster, silhouetted by the glow of the flare. "This guy doesn't know shit," he said, pointing at Kyle. "He's a fucking liar. All he's got is a bunch of hearsay off the web and a hand-drawn map."

Chloe took hold of Luke's sleeve. "Calm down. Just sit down over there and be still."

Luke glared at her, and for a moment, she thought he would hit her. He blew out an exasperated breath and stomped over beside Jared, unshouldering his backpack.

"I'm sorry, guys," Kyle said. "I know I kind of. . .

misrepresented how much I knew about this place." He pulled on his goatee. "But I *am* a good caver. I'm experienced. I never would have brought you all in here if I thought there was a real danger someone might get hurt."

"It wasn't Kyle's fault my damn knee gave out on me," Jared said. "He didn't know. I should've been more careful. I should have watched where I was stepping."

"It's not your fault, either," Luke said. He uncapped a bottle of water and took a swallow. "Numbnuts here shouldn't have led us into that shit."

"Nobody forced you to come," Kyle said. "You could have stayed outside."

"Yeah, with a damn bobcat or whatever ripped the guts out of that animal we found."

"Guys, let's just take a rest and head back out of here," Brandon said. "I think we've all seen enough."

"I agree," Chloe said. She sank down next to Luke and pulled off her backpack. Her stomach was growling and she remembered she'd picked up some trail mix at the QuikStop.

"Kyle did all this for free, you know," Brandon said to Luke. "Provided all the equipment, got us out here. You could be a little more appreciative."

Luke glared at him. "Shut up, Brandon. Nobody wants to hear your faggot shit."

Chloe froze, her fingers poised to open the bag of trail mix. Her breath left her.

Brandon's face turned ghostly white. She could see it, even in the dim light. His eyes narrowed. "What did you say?"

Luke took a swig of water. "Come on, Brandon.

You're gay, aren't you? We all know. You're not fooling anybody. Is he, Chloe?"

Brandon looked at Chloe, his eyes round and hurt. Chloe's heart sank in her chest. She shook her head. "Brandon, I never said anything, I swear."

He continued to stare at her. "You *knew*?"

Her mouth was like sandpaper. "No," she said. "I mean. . ."

"Hell, we all know," Luke said. "I knew when you and Chloe kept hanging around and you never tried to put the make on her that something was wrong with you."

"Shut up, Luke," Jared said. "Just shut your fucking mouth."

Brandon looked around at all of them, shaking his head.

Kyle came up beside him. "Hey. . . "

Brandon held up his hand and walked away from them into the darkness. He sank down against one of the stalagmites and doused his headlamp.

Chloe glared at Luke. "What the hell's wrong with you?"

"Hey, I just said what we were all thinking," Luke said. He put the water bottle to his lips and took a long drink.

Chloe blew out a breath and climbed to her feet. She took one last glance at Luke and made her way toward Brandon.

Behind her, Jared said, "You're an asshole, Luke."

Brandon was sitting with his legs drawn up, his head between his knees. Chloe could see tears glinting on his cheeks. "Hey," she said.

"Hey."

"Wanna talk?"

"Not really."

She sat down beside him. "Luke's an asswipe. You know that, right?"

Brandon stared straight ahead. "Looked like you were getting along with him pretty good."

Chloe sighed and ripped open her trail mix. She held the bag out to Brandon. He opened up his hand and she poured some into his palm. "He's been after me a long time."

"I know," Brandon said. He gathered some of the mix in his fingers and dropped it into his mouth. "I thought you had better judgment than that."

"All I did was hold his hand," she said. "I didn't sleep with him. I didn't even kiss him."

Brandon munched the trail mix. "I'm sorry. I don't know why it bothered me."

"He was just here," Chloe said. "I needed someone to walk with me. You seemed. . . I don't know, preoccupied with Kyle." Brandon buried his face in his hands, and Chloe immediately felt she'd said the wrong thing. "So. . . are you and Kyle. . . "

"No," Brandon said, his voice muffled. "He's straight. We're just friends."

"I see."

He turned and looked at her, resting his head on his knee. "Nobody knows about me," he said. "At least, nobody was *supposed* to know. Hell, my parents don't even know. My mother will go ballistic if she finds out."

"I won't tell anyone."

"But how did Luke know? Did he mean what he said? Have you all known all along?"

Chloe stared at the pulsating light of the flare behind the rock formations. "I think we all suspected, but nobody *knew*." She looked at him. "I take that back. I think deep down I *did* know. Some part of me has always known. But it just wasn't a big deal to me."

Brandon pulled off his helmet and pressed his forehead against his knees. "I didn't want to come out. Not yet. I just wasn't ready."

Chloe put an arm around his shoulders. "Look, Brandon. Nobody cares if you're gay. It doesn't change how we feel about you."

"But Luke – "

"Look at me."

Brandon turned and stared at her.

"Luke's a fuckwad. Okay?"

Brandon chuckled and wiped his eyes. "I know."

"You're still my friend. We'll still hang out. Do all the crap we've always done together. Nothing's changed. Okay?"

Brandon nodded. "Okay." He set the helmet back on his head.

Chloe tossed back a handful of trail mix and stretched. "I'm ready to get the hell out of here and head back to civilization," she said, her mouth full. She stood and offered her hand. "You coming?"

Brandon took a deep breath and switched his lamp back on. "I'm coming." He took Chloe's hand and pulled himself to his feet.

22

KASSIDY

Kassidy continued massaging Jared's knee. "How's it feel?"

He nodded. "Better."

He took a sip of water and leaned his head back against the rocky wall. His knee felt swollen under her fingers, and she wondered if he had done more damage than he thought. Wondered if he was in far more pain than he was letting on. It terrified her. She thought of making the trek back through the narrow passage and crawling back through the tunnel, of the long walk back to the car and wondered how he was going to make it.

Beside her, Luke was tearing into a Butterfinger. "Think we should splint up your leg or something?" he said to Jared.

Jared looked at him. "With what?"

"I don't know. Maybe Kyle's got something. Or maybe a couple of us could go out and find something and bring it back in."

"I'll be all right," Jared said. But his face was pale and drawn.

Brandon and Chloe appeared out of the darkness. "How's the knee?" Chloe said.

Jared managed a weak smile. "I'll live."

Kassidy glanced at Brandon. He stood behind Chloe, staring at the ground, not looking at any of them. God, she felt bad for him. Luke was such a fucking jerk. She couldn't believe she had let herself start falling for him. Seeing him take Chloe's hand back at the gift shop had given her a stab of hurt. But what he'd said to Brandon was too much.

Luke had taken off his helmet and his sweaty hair stood up in spikes. He was crunching candy and leaning back against the wall and looking so damned sexy and she hated the fact that she was turned on by him. Hated that even after the awful things he'd said to Brandon she would still ravage him right here if she had the chance.

He caught her looking at him and stopped chewing. "What?"

She shook her head. "Nothing."

Luke swallowed and craned to peer around Chloe. "Brandon, I'm sorry, dude. I shouldn't have said that."

"Just forget it," Brandon said. His voice was small.

"I mean, I don't care," Luke went on. "None of us care. It's your business, what you want to do."

Chloe blew out a breath. "Just stop talking, Luke."

He threw up his hands. "Fine."

They all looked at each other for a moment in awkward silence, and finally Jared said, "Are we about ready to get out of here?"

Kassidy touched his knee lightly. "You sure you can

make it?"

"I can't stay here."

"We can carry you out," Luke said. "That passage-way and that little tunnel might be tough, but Brandon and I can get you back to the car."

Kassidy thought of the cellphone in her backpack. "Maybe we should call 911. If nothing else we can get an emergency crew down here to get you out."

Chloe was holding up her phone for them to see. "You checked yours? There's no signal down here."

"Somebody could go back outside and get to where there *is* a signal, though," Brandon said.

Jared held up his hands. "Guys, I'll be fine. I can make it. Let's just get out of here. I'll be all right."

Luke got to his feet and put the helmet back on his head. "Yo, chief!"

Behind them, Kyle sat on an outcropping of rock, turning a flashlight over and over in his hands. "You talking to me?"

"Yeah, I'm talking to you," Luke said. "Let's blow this popsicle stand and get the fuck out of here."

Kyle made his way toward them, shoving the flash-light into his backpack. "Sure."

Kassidy got to her knees and took hold of Jared's arm. "Can you stand up, baby?" She looked at Luke. "Help me, here."

The two of them got Jared to his feet and helped him limp toward the passageway.

Kyle adjusted his pack and switched on his lamp. "You gonna make it, man?"

Jared was leaning heavily on Kassidy's shoulders. He was so heavy. It was taking everything she had to hold him up. "Brandon," she gasped, "you're going to have to do this."

Brandon was there at once. He took Jared's arm and draped it over his shoulders. "We'll get you out of here," he said.

"It hurts worse than I thought," Jared said, his voice only a whisper.

"Just take it nice and slow," Luke said.

Jared took another step and cried out. Only Luke and Brandon kept him from collapsing. "I've got to sit," he said. "I can't do it, I can't do it."

Luke and Brandon lowered him to the ground. "We're gonna have to call in some help," Luke said.

Kassidy could feel panic rising in her chest. "Someone's got to get out and call 911."

"I'll go," Kyle said, and they all looked at him. "I'm the most experienced. It'll be quicker."

"No arguments there," Luke said.

"I'm coming with you," Brandon said.

Kyle looked at him. "I don't know if that's a good idea."

"Please," Brandon said.

Something seemed to pass between the two of them, and then Kyle nodded. "All right." He wriggled out of his backpack. "We'll leave our packs here, though, and just take our phones."

Brandon nodded, setting his pack down then digging his phone out of it.

"You guys be careful," Chloe said.

"We will," Brandon told her.

"Let's go," Kyle said, hooking a thumb back toward the passage.

Brandon took one last look at them and ducked out of sight.

23
BRANDON

Moving through the passageway was easier without the added weight of the backpack, but it was still tough going. Brandon followed Kyle along the highway of spray-painted arrows, feeling the sweat already trickling along his scalp.

Kyle looked back over his shoulder. "You okay back there, hoss?"

"Yep."

"Let me know if I'm going too fast for you."

Brandon watched Kyle move deftly between the rock walls and wished he could say something to take away what Luke had said. Brandon had seen something in Kyle's eyes – disappointment, betrayal. It was hard to say. But he knew things were never going to be the same between them again.

Hell, things were never going to be the same between him and *any* of the others, now that they knew. Except Chloe. She had always been the only one who seemed to understand him. It was a shame he wasn't straight; they would have made a good couple.

"Hey, man," Kyle said, still plodding forward. "About all that shit Luke said. . . "

Oh, hell, here it comes. "Yeah," Brandon said. "Sorry about that."

"No need for you to apologize," Kyle said. "Luke's an asshole. I just hated it for you, man." He stopped and turned around. "But just so you know, I'm not gay."

Brandon couldn't meet Kyle's eyes. "I know. I don't want you to think. . . "

Kyle put a hand on Brandon's shoulder. "It's all right, dude. It doesn't matter to me. I don't think it matters to any of those people back there. Even Luke."

Brandon could feel his face growing hot. His ears were burning up. "I just didn't want it come out like that. And I was afraid you'd get the wrong idea."

Kyle shook his head. "Like I said, doesn't matter to me. I can still be your friend. But I can't be your boyfriend."

"I understand."

"I don't swing that way."

"I got it." Honestly, his ears felt like they would burst into flames. Why wouldn't Kyle just shut up?

Kyle smiled. "You know the funny thing? I was thinking about introducing you to my sister."

Brandon laughed. He finally looked at Kyle, into those eyes he'd thought about so many nights. "Sorry if I made you uncomfortable."

Kyle gave him one last pat on the shoulder. "It's all right, hoss. We're good." He turned and headed into the darkness ahead.

Brandon followed. He wasn't sure how to feel about all this. He was disappointed. Ashamed. Angry. Crushed. He had known all along he couldn't have that kind of relationship with Kyle. But keeping it to himself had meant he wouldn't get hurt by reality, that he could enjoy being with Kyle and satisfy himself vicariously through fantasy. Now the fantasy was dead, along with the imagined hope it brought with it.

In a way it was liberating. The whole thing was liberating. He no longer had to pretend around any of them. He was free to pursue a real relationship. With a real guy, not a far-flung daydream.

Now all he had to do was tell his parents. And the thought of that made his blood turn to ice.

"Careful," Kyle said. "We're back at the loose stuff. Watch your footing."

Brandon stepped gingerly onto the rock. "Why's it different here?"

"Just a vein of sandstone through the middle of the limestone. You see it sometimes, especially in this area. That's why I want to study geology. I love this kind of stuff. If I can – " He stopped abruptly in mid-step.

Brandon froze. "Kyle? What's wrong?"

He heard a soft click, a small pebble skittering down the face of the rock.

Kyle slowly turned. His face was ashen. "We need to get out of here. Right now." He nudged Brandon backwards. "Turn around slowly and head back."

Brandon's bowels felt loose. "What's wrong."

Kyle's voice was firm, yet barely audible. "Now."

Before Brandon could move, a whispering sound came from above them. Dust was raining down onto their helmets.

Kyle's eyes were wide with panic. "Now!" He shoved Brandon back.

Brandon went flying, landing hard on the rocky floor. Kyle disappeared in a cascade of rocks and dust. Brandon shielded his face against the onslaught and braced himself for an impact that never came. After an eternity, the roar of falling debris stopped, punctuated with the clatter of a few more stones.

For a moment, all Brandon could do was writhe on the floor, gasping for the breath that had been knocked out of him. His back screamed in pain and his head hummed where the helmet had slammed into the rock floor. Finally – mercifully – his lungs began to fill with air, but the cloud of dirt in the tunnel was chokingly thick. He opened his eyes and could see nothing but eddies of dust and silt swirling in the beam of his head-lamp. He managed to maneuver onto his hands and knees, coughing and gagging in the heavy air. He crawled forward, then collapsed on the rocks. He was not surprised to taste the metal tang of blood on his lips. "Kyle!"

He sat up, and a sharp pain in his side nearly took him down to the ground. He wondered if he had broken a rib. "Kyle! Where are you?"

The sweatshirt, though ripped in a couple of places, had protected his arms. He ran a hand across his face and wiped away blood. He touched his fingers to his cheek and felt a small gash just below his eye. He had been lucky.

"Kyle!"

Then he saw, and blinding panic gave way to disbe-lief.

The tunnel had collapsed. The way out was completely blocked. Worse, an arm stretched from beneath the rubble, an arm coated with blood and dust. An arm with a wolf tattoo.

"Kyle!"

Brandon inched toward the arm, sliding on the loose rocks, and grabbed the hand. It was still warm but unresponsive. He sat holding it. Looking at it. He felt numb. Even the pain in his back and side seemed far away. For an instant he hoped Kyle was still alive, that somehow he had miraculously survived the collapse, that he was caught in some kind of pocket of air beneath the rubble. He began to dig frantically, stopping only when he realized he might cause the rock and debris to tumble down upon him.

He had to get back to the others.

24
LUKE

For one brief moment, Luke thought he was hallucinating, that he was seeing the ghost of some long-forgotten miner stumbling out of the dark – all bloody and disheveled. But when the figure crumpled not ten feet away, he realized it was Brandon.

He rushed to him and knelt beside him. "Brandon! What the hell!"

"The tunnel collapsed," Brandon sputtered. "I think. . . I think Kyle's dead."

Someone – Chloe or Kassidy – gave a small shriek.

"What happened?" Jared said.

Brandon swallowed. "That place back there, that area he said wasn't stable. We'd just got to it when the top gave way. He shoved me out of the way just in time." He made a choking sound and Luke realized he was crying. "He shoved me out of the way."

Chloe stood. Her eyes were round and glistening. "Are you sure he's not just hurt? Or trapped?"

"He's dead!" Brandon screamed. "He's dead! I saw him!" He covered his dirt-streaked face and sobbed into his hands.

Luke motioned to the backpacks. "Chloe, bring him some water." He took the bottle from her and uncapped it, then handed it to Brandon. "Here, drink this."

Brandon took a sip, then handed it back to Luke. "We can't get out," Brandon cried. "The tunnel's completely blocked. We're trapped in here."

Kassidy covered her mouth. "Oh, my God."

Chloe sank to her knees next to Brandon and put an arm around him. "There's got to be a way through there. Maybe if we all get in there and start digging – "

"We might cause a second collapse," Luke said. He stood and paced back and forth. "Jesus Christ, what are we gonna do?"

"We can't stay here," Kassidy said, her voice rising in pitch. "We've got to get out."

Luke chewed his thumbnail. "We need to check out the passageway. I want to see for myself."

Brandon grabbed his leg. "No! You can't go back in there. It's too dangerous."

"Brandon's right," Jared said.

Luke pulled from Brandon's grasp and unzipped his backpack. He pulled out the flashlight he had stuck in it earlier. "I'm going. I'll come right back." He looked at all of them. "Anyone coming with me?"

Chloe stood. "I will," she said, and Luke felt a warmth spread through him.

"Chloe, don't," Brandon said.

"We'll be fine," Chloe told him. "We'll stick together." She stood and looked at Luke. "Ready?"

"Let's do it," he said, leading the way toward the

passage.

"For God's sake, be careful," Kassidy called to them, her voice cracking.

Luke inched his way into the crevice, pointing the flashlight ahead like a sword. Behind him, Chloe was grasping the fingers on his other hand. Together they moved through the tunnel, both of them barely breathing. Luke weighed his steps carefully. Dust still swirled in the air, and he tensed every time his arm brushed the passage wall.

This would probably rank in the top five of stupid things he had done. But he had to see. They had to know. Brandon was nearly hysterical. Maybe he was so panicked he wasn't thinking straight. And if Kyle was still alive and hurt, they had to do something to help him.

"How much farther?" Chloe asked.

"I think we're almost there," Luke said.

Truthfully, he didn't know. The air was so thick with dust he could see only a couple of feet in front of him. He tried to blink the grit from his eyes, but they felt dirty and gummy.

His feet hit loose rock and he stopped. "Be careful," he said. He shined the light ahead, but the beam seemed to reflect back into his eyes off the dust.

"See anything?"

"I can't see shit." He turned back to her. "Stay here. I'm going ahead."

"The hell you are," Chloe said, tightening her grip on his hand. "I'm coming with you."

He couldn't help but smile. "All right."

They inched forward across the gravel and turned a slight bend. The path disappeared into a pile of rubble.

He shined the light toward the ceiling of the passage. There was no way over the pile. No way around it. Brandon was right. They were trapped.

Luke shined the light around the bottom of the pile and the beam caught something. A bloodied arm jutted from beneath the rock. "Oh, fuck."

"What?" Chloe said, her voice thick.

"Don't look," he told her.

"Is it Kyle?"

"Yeah."

Chloe let out a small breath. "Is he. . . ?"

"Yeah. I'm pretty sure." He swallowed and turned back to her. "Let's go back. There's no way through."

They had just stepped back around the bend when a rumble came from behind them. Luke swung the light just in time to see more rock and debris tumbling down and a wall of dust rushing at them. He shoved Chloe's back against the wall, shielding her with his body. After an eternity, when the tunnel was quiet again, he eased off her. She was gazing at him, her dark eyes filled with tears, her face streaked with dirt. He felt a sudden urge to kiss her, not in a sexual way, but to give her reassurance, to show her everything would be all right. That they would make it out of here.

"It'll be okay," he said. "We're gonna be okay."

25
KASSIDY

When Kassidy saw Luke and Chloe emerge from the passage, she stood and let out a breath it seemed she'd been holding since they left. They were both covered in dust. Chloe had been crying.

"Completely blocked," Luke said. "Brandon was right."

"Kyle?" Jared asked.

Luke shook his head.

Kassidy felt numb and cold. "Then we're really trapped," she said, and her voice seemed lost in the darkness.

"Surely someone will come along," Chloe said. "Someone will see the vehicles – "

"Who?" Luke said. "We're parked half a mile off the main road. Nobody will come down that far, not on Sunday. It could be a week before anybody finds our cars."

"People will miss us," Kassidy said. "When we

don't show up for class or work. . ."

Jared reached up and grabbed her hand. "How will they know where to look, Kass?" He looked around at them. "I didn't bother telling anybody else we were coming out here. Did any of you?"

They all looked at each other, no one daring to speak. Behind them, the flare gave a last sputter and died, plunging the rest of the cave into utter blackness. Kassidy felt panic seize her gut. She sank back down against Jared.

"There's got to be another way out of here," Luke said. He looked at Brandon. "That map Kyle had. Did he have it with him?"

"I saw him stick it in his pocket," Brandon said.

"Maybe he had another copy," Chloe said.

Luke was already hefting Kyle's backpack into the circle of light from their helmets. "Let's see what he's got in here." He unzipped the flap and pulled out a coil of nylon rope, followed by several metal carabiners, anchors, and other devices Kassidy didn't recognize. "Hey," he said, pulling out a small plastic box. "First aid kit."

Chloe took it from him and opened it. "Let's clean up some of these cuts," she said to Brandon. She opened a small bottle, doused a gauze pad with its contents and began dabbing the bloody gash underneath Brandon's eye. Brandon winced.

Luke pawed through the rest of the pack's contents. "Snacks, a couple of bottles of water, matches. Couple more of those flares. A candle." He blew out a breath. "That's it. No map."

Kassidy's fingers began to tingle. Her hands were shaking. "What are we gonna do? We can't stay in here. We've got to get out of here." She looked at Jared, feeling her eyes well up with tears again. "We've got to get out of here."

He reached for her, and his hands were warm and dry. "Calm down, Kass. We'll get out."

She squeezed his hands in hers. "What if we don't?" The panic was in her chest now. Her heart hammered against her ribs. "We'll die in here. We'll die!"

Jared's eyes narrowed. He pulled his hands out of her grasp and took her by the shoulders. "Stop it," he said, his voice even but firm. "You'll give yourself an anxiety attack." He looked into her eyes. "Breathe."

She tried to will her heart to slow down, but it beat faster. Her breath came in short, gasping gulps. She looked into Jared's eyes, but it was like looking at him down a long tunnel.

A cave.

She felt her body falling backwards. She seemed to drop forever into the darkness.

And then she was lying on the cave floor and opening her eyes to see a circle of headlamps shining down on her.

"What happened?" Chloe said.

"She passed out," Jared said. "I think she had a panic attack."

Kassidy struggled to sit up as Chloe knelt beside her. Her head swam. "I think I'm all right," she said.

"You need some water?" Chloe asked.

Kassidy shook her head. She wasn't thirsty at all. But her bladder was full and aching. "I've got to pee," she said.

Chloe pulled her to her feet. "Come on," she said. "We'll go over there behind those rocks." She led her to a small grotto, out of sight of the guys. "You go back there and pee. I'll stand guard."

For some reason, that sounded funny, and Kassidy suppressed a giggle.

The area was shielded from the others, but was open to a wide area lined with stalagmites. The headlamp barely illuminated anything past them, and how deep or long the space was, she couldn't tell.

She slid her jeans and panties down her legs and crouched. She knew of cave crickets and bats and other creatures that might be in here, and the thoughts of something brushing her bare skin with its tiny hairy legs sent a shiver through her. Urine trickled onto the floor, and she could feel waves of heat from it against her bare buttocks. Her bladder relaxed with relief.

Jared was right. They would get out of here. They just had to find the way. And there had to be another way. There just had to.

She stood and pulled up her jeans and then froze. Something had just scuttled out of the range of the light. She saw it, a darker shadow against the blackness beyond, and then it was gone. A faint sound reached her ears, a slight clicking that sounded like. . . *claws*.

"Chloe!"

"Right here, girl."

"Did you hear that?"

"I didn't hear anything."

Kassidy zipped up her jeans. "I thought I heard something moving. You didn't see anything, did you?"

Chloe poked her head around the rock. "I didn't see anything or hear anything."

Kassidy took a deep breath. The panic was returning. She pointed behind them. "Look through there. Is anything back there?"

Chloe stuck her head between two stalagmites. The beam from her headlamp swept back and forth through the blackness. "There's nothing there." She reached out and pulled Kassidy close. "Let's get back to the others."

26
JARED

Jared's knee was swollen. It strained against the fabric of his jeans, and it hurt like fuck, almost as bad as that night on the football field. There was no way he was going to be able to walk out of here. He would have to wait for help. The others would have to leave him behind while they went to look for a way out.

Chloe and Kassidy returned and Kassidy nestled into the crook of his arm. She still seemed shaky, and Jared was worried about her. He'd seen her have a panic attack one other time, during finals week, but it had been nothing like this. She hadn't passed out that time. They'd laughed it off then, joking about college stress. But just now he had seen something in her eyes he hadn't before, an absolute, blinding panic. Almost as if she had lost complete control of her other senses. He wrapped his arm tighter around her. "Feel better?"

"I'm so cold," she said. She drew her knees up and crossed her arms across her chest. "I wish I had something hot to drink. Cocoa or coffee."

"Coffee would be great," Luke said. He took a seat on the cave floor and crossed his ankles. "When we get out of here, the first thing I'm gonna do is get me a cup."

Jared took a sip of his water. "A mocha latte from Starbucks sure sounds good right now."

"What is wrong with you people?" Brandon said, pacing back and forth. "Kyle is dead. He's dead! And you're talking about fucking *coffee*!" He covered his face and wept.

Chloe put her arms around him. "It's gonna be okay, Brandon." She pulled him to the floor with the others. "Sit down."

Brandon wiped his face on his sleeve. "I'm sorry," he said. "I just. . . Kyle. . . and. . . " Tears rolled down his cheeks. "And I couldn't help him. I couldn't help him."

Chloe patted his back. "We know, baby, we know. No one's blaming you. There wasn't anything you could do."

They sat in a circle, watching each other and listening to Brandon cry. Jared was numb with fear. He had no idea what they were going to do, or how they were going to get out of here.

Finally, Luke leaned forward. "The way I see it, we've only got one choice, and that's to find those doors where we first tried to come in."

"But they're locked," Kassidy said. "How are we gonna get through there?"

"They're not locked, they're chained," Luke said. "And they opened outward, toward the visitor center. And if me and Brandon both pushed hard enough – "

"You might could break those chains," Jared finished for him. A glimmer of hope sparked in his chest.

"But how do we know which way to go?" Chloe said. "We have no idea where we are now."

"Kyle said we're in the main cave," Luke said. He swept an arm around. "This must have been part of the tour. I'll bet if we follow this passage we're bound to reach the entrance."

Jared looked past them, into the blackness beyond. "When we crawled in through that tunnel, the visitor's center was up that hill to our right. Assuming we didn't get completely turned backwards through those passageways, the center should *still* be to our right." He pointed toward where the floor of the cave seemed to slope upward. "That way."

Luke nodded. "You're right."

"Well, what are we waiting for?" Kassidy said. "Let's head that way."

"What about Jared?" Brandon said. "He can't make it that far."

Jared blew out a breath. "He's right, guys. I can barely make it a few steps. There's no way I can make it up through there."

"Brandon and I can carry you," Luke said. "One on each side."

Jared shook his head. "You know that won't work. Besides, it'll be quicker if you all go on without me and call for help."

"We can't just leave you," Brandon said. "Maybe just one of us could go."

"We'll need all the strength we can muster to break the chains on those doors," Luke told him. "At the very least, you and I have to go."

"I'll stay here with Jared," Kassidy said. "The rest

of you go on."

"I can stay, too," Chloe said.

Kassidy shook her head. "No, you go with them, Chloe. Those two clowns will get lost without a woman's help."

Jared looked at her. "You don't have to stay, you know. I'll be all right."

She stared into his eyes. "I'm not leaving you," she said. "Not now. Not ever."

Luke was packing the contents of Kyle's pack into his own. "We'll take his stuff with us," he said. "I don't know what half this shit is, but we may need it."

"Hey," Jared said, and Luke looked at him. "You guys be careful. Stay together."

Luke smacked him on the shoulder. "We will."

27

CHLOE

Chloe looked back as they mounted the slope. She could see Kassidy and Jared sitting together in the small pool of light from their headlamps. They looked so insignificant in the midst of the black vastness around them. Then the light disappeared and they were gone. Luke had warned them about conserving the battery power for the lamps, as no one knew how long it would take to reach the front of the cave, get through the doors and call for help. It could be hours. Chloe shivered. She certainly didn't envy them sitting in pitch darkness all that time. But at least they had each other.

She was so glad Kassidy decided to come today. And from the looks of it, Kassidy was glad, too. She had no idea what had been going through Kassidy's head, or why she had treated Jared badly for so long. But she thought of the way Kassidy had stared at Luke at the convenience store when she thought no one was watching, and she wondered if Kassidy had tried to start something with him. Maybe he had led her on, let her think something would happen between the two of them. Maybe he had strung her along just like she had strung Jared along. And that look today. The way she gazed at him with a mixture of sorrow and longing. If Luke had turned her away and hurt her, it served her right. She didn't deserve any less.

Chloe focused her attention on Luke's legs in front of her. What if he did the same thing to her? Played her and got her into bed and then tossed her aside. She had waited so long to give herself to a man; she didn't think she could bear that.

The slope leveled out and they were passing through a narrower passage. Formations resembling melted wax surrounded them, and their headlamps cast eerie shadows across the walls of the cave behind. She thought of what she had seen earlier when they had first come into the cave – something stirring just outside the rim of light. And then Kassidy saying she thought she heard something moving around. "Luke," Chloe said, "do you think there are any animals living in here?"

"Probably nothing but a few bats. Like Kyle said."

Of course. Bats. As much as she hated them, the thought that what she and Kassidy may have encountered had only been bats gave her a strange sense of comfort. Nasty as they were, bats couldn't eat you. They couldn't rip your guts out like that animal outside. Whatever it had been. She shivered again.

"You okay?" Brandon said behind her.

"I'm fine."

"I'm sorry about all this, guys," he said. "We wouldn't be in this shit if it hadn't been for me."

"What're you talking about?" Luke said. "You

didn't make the tunnel collapse."

"But coming out here with Kyle was my idea."

Luke stopped and turned to look at him. "Stop it. It's nobody's fault. Quit blaming yourself. It's just getting on my nerves." He took off again, and Chloe and Brandon followed.

"You really think we can break through those doors?" Chloe said.

"We've got to try," Luke said. If nothing else, maybe we'll be close enough to the surface that we can get a cell signal."

"What if we can't get through?" Brandon said.

Luke didn't answer.

28

KASSIDY

The others had been gone for a while now, leaving Kassidy and Jared alone in the black silence. The dark seemed to close in upon them like a fist. Kassidy could feel it tightening around her, squeezing her.

She lay next to Jared, her head against his chest, feeling it rise and fall, hearing the steady beat of his heart, and holding onto him as if he would disappear if she stopped touching him. As if the darkness would swallow him whole.

"How long do you think they'll be gone?" she asked. She said it more to break the deafening silence than anything. She knew he didn't know. Nobody knew.

"Not long," he said.

She smiled. "You always were a terrible liar."

"Is that why you wanted to break up with me?"

She blew out a breath. She didn't want to get into this again. Not here. Not now. "Yes," she said. "That's it. You were always telling me how good I looked and I knew you were lying about it."

He laughed humorlessly. "Seriously. Why, Kass? Did I do something wrong? Did I hurt you?"

She had no idea how to answer that. "It wasn't anything you did."

"I see."

"It was more like I didn't know what I wanted. I thought I wanted something else. But now I know I was wrong."

He took a deep breath. "Was there – *is* there – someone else? Tell me the truth."

It was easier in the dark when she couldn't see his eyes boring into her. When she couldn't see the pained expression on his face. "There was," she said. "But not now." And it was the truth. It was over, if anything had even been there to begin with.

"It was Luke, wasn't it?"

She felt her body go rigid and her eyes wept fresh tears. "How did you know?"

He sighed. "The same way we all figured out Brandon was gay. It's obvious. Every time he's around you light up like a candle."

"I didn't mean for it to happen," she said, feeling the tears run down her face. She could taste the salt on her lips.

He struggled to sit up, and she let go of him. He pushed away from her. "How could the two of you do that?" he said. "You carried on right under my nose."

"It only happened once," she said.

He grunted. "Once is enough."

"It's *over*, Jared. Believe me. There's nothing else going on between us. He's after Chloe, you know that."

"I know he was with some other girl last night," he said, and she felt a stab of hurt. "He's a player, Kassidy. You of all people should know that."

"I *do* know that. It's why there could never be anything between us." She felt for his hand and took hold of it. "I love you, Jared. Even if I thought I didn't, I know now that I do."

"You cheated on me," he said. "You fucking *cheated* on me." He jerked his hand away. "I can't ever trust you again."

"Don't do this, Jared. Don't do this now."

"I really thought we had something special, you know? I thought we'd get married someday. Raise a family."

The ache in her chest was almost more than she could bear. "I'm so sorry," she said. She wiped her face with her hands. "If you'd just listen to me. If you'd just – "

"Just shut up, Kassidy. Just shut the fuck up."

29
LUKE

They had been walking forever. No one had said anything for a long time. The exertion and the stress had left them all drained.

There had been several crudely painted wooden signs along the way, names of various formations. *The Devil's Dining Table*, a large rock with a sheer, flat surface. A tall humanoid shape standing like a sentinel called *The Stone Giant*. *The Wedding Chapel*, with its intricate, lacy canopy of mottled rock draped over a small grotto. All had no doubt been dramatically lit during the cavern's heyday, and even now Luke caught glimpses of ancient electrical cables still snaked through the rock. They were on the right track. He knew it.

The passage had again widened out, then narrowed and sloped upward. Here there were handrails along the path colored orange with rust, and a staircase that seemed to have been carved out of the limestone. "Careful," Luke said.

At the top of the steps the passageway opened up into another wide open area. Wooden benches were set up in rows facing a man-made stage.

"Where are we?" Brandon said.

Chloe looked around. "Looks like some kind of amphitheater."

"We must be getting close to the entrance," Luke said. His pulse quickened. Behind the expanse of benches he could see the tunnel curving to the left. "Come on."

30
JARED

He listened to Kassidy crying in the dark next to him and his stomach burned. To think she and Luke had something going on right in front of him. Even while Luke pretended to be his best friend, sharing an apartment with him and playing video games with him and telling him all about his conquests. And while Jared was sleeping in Kassidy's bed, she was dreaming of Luke. Had she been thinking about Luke Friday night when Jared was making love to her?

He felt completely sickened. Why hadn't he seen it before now? All those little glances between the two of them. All those times Kassidy had brushed her hands against Luke casually, "accidentally." And what had she said this morning, that she had been thinking about breaking up for six months. Jesus Christ. He had been a fool.

He felt Kassidy tense up beside him. "Did you hear that?"

"What?"

"Listen."

He held his breath, straining to hear above the pounding of his heart in his ears. Then he heard it – a soft whimper coming from the direction the others had gone. "What is that?"

She put her hand on his arm and shushed him.

The sound came again, a little louder this time. It was almost like –

"Somebody's calling for help," Kassidy said. "Somebody's hurt." She switched on her headlamp and he blinked in the sudden blinding light.

They sat still as statues, not daring to move or breathe. Then the voice came again, thin and desperate, somewhere in the darkness: "Kassidy, help me."

"Oh, my God," Kassidy said, getting to her feet. "That's Chloe." She headed toward the voice, her light shining into the nothingness in front of her.

31
BRANDON

Around the bend from the amphitheater, the path ended. They had reached the cave entrance and the steel doors.

"No," Chloe said. "No, no, no."

The doors were covered with a metal grate. It was welded to the steel frame.

Luke reached out his hand to it and felt along the woven metal. "Dammit!" he cried. He banged his fist against the grate. "God*dammit!*"

This couldn't be real. "Maybe we can get it off of there," Brandon said. He looped his fingers through the mesh. "Help me."

Luke and Chloe grabbed on as well, pushing and pulling at the unyielding metal. The grate was solid. It wasn't moving.

Luke kicked the mesh and sank to the floor. He took off his helmet and ran his sleeve across his face. "Fuck."

"What do we do now?" Chloe said, her voice shaky.

Luke shook his head and combed his fingers through his hair. "I guess we go back and tell Kassidy and Jared we've got to find another way out."

"Wait!" Chloe wriggled out of her back pack and dug into it. "Our phones. See if you can get a signal."

Brandon thrust his hand into the pocket of the coveralls and grabbed his phone. The screen was cracked and lifeless. It had no doubt been broken when the tunnel collapsed.

"I got nothing," Luke said.

"Me, too," Chloe said. She shoved the phone back into the pack. "Well, I guess that's it, then."

An idea struck Brandon so simple and so clear, he wondered why they hadn't thought of it before. "What about the river?"

"What river?" Luke said.

"The river that flows through the cave," Brandon said. "The one they used to give boat tours on. We find the river and we can follow it right out."

Chloe's face lit up. "Brandon, you're a genius."

Luke stuck his helmet back on. "How do we find it?"

"Same way we got here," Brandon said. "We start walking. Let's get back and tell Kassidy and Jared the new plan."

32
KASSIDY

Kassidy moved through the darkness, sweeping her light back and forth among the rocks. "Chloe! Where are you?"

What in the name of God had happened to them? If Chloe was hurt and calling for help, then something must have gone wrong. Luke and Brandon might be lying hurt somewhere else. Or worse. "Chloe!"

A faint voice came out of the darkness off to her right. "Kassidy."

Kassidy turned toward the sound. "Chloe?"

"Over here."

A small passageway angled off the main corridor. She must be in there. "Are you hurt? What's wrong? What happened?"

"Help me."

Kassidy stepped off the path and headed toward the opening. Just inside, the passage narrowed. She could see nothing ahead but the jagged limestone walls.

"Chloe, are you in here?"

"Help me, Kassidy."

The headlamp flickered.

No. Please God, no.

She moved farther into the passage. The headlamp flickered again, then dimmed. She reached up and tapped it. It brightened slightly. "Chloe, my light's about to go out!" She felt her pockets and felt the flashlight Kyle had given her up top. Good. It was still there.

"Kassidy, please!"

"I'm coming. What's wrong?"

There was a bend ahead. Kassidy stumbled across a small pile of rubble and looked down. It wasn't rubble. She stared at it, not believing what she was seeing. It was a pile of bones. They were large. Like human bones. "Chloe? *Chloe!*"

Something moved just ahead. Something white.

"Chloe is that you? What are you doing in here?"

The headlamp flickered and went out. *Shit!* She reached up and tapped it again. Nothing. She pulled the small flashlight from her pocket and flicked it on.

A large white dog stood before her, its black eyes locked onto hers. It opened its mouth. "Kassidy, help me," it said in Chloe's voice.

Kassidy backed up. No. This couldn't be real. She was dreaming. Seeing things. This couldn't be real. It couldn't be.

"*No!*"

Her heel caught against a rock and she spiraled backwards. The flashlight went flying from her hand and she heard the crack of plastic shattering against rock. Somewhere in the dark, the dog growled. It was moving closer.

"Jared!" she screamed. "*Jared!*"

The weight of paws was suddenly upon her chest, and it growled in her ear. She could feel the heat of the thing's rancid breath on her neck.

She pushed her hands in front of her, shoving the heavy bundle of fur off to the side. Screaming, she scrambled to her feet. But in the darkness she was completely disoriented. Her helmet banged against the wall.

The headlamp sprang to life, illuminating the dog in her path.

No! How had it gotten *behind* her?

As she watched in horror, the dog seemed to grow, to swell. Blood appeared in the white fur along its back. It shook, as if having a seizure. Its black eyes were glazed and unfocused. A ridge appeared in the dog's skull, and with a crack it split in two, spraying the walls with blood. And then something was coming out of it. Something else was emerging from the dog. Something with a long wolf-like snout and sharp yellow teeth. And black, black eyes. Soulless eyes.

The bloody carcass of the dog fell away from it as it rose to its full height, towering above her. "Kassidy," it said.

And then it was upon her.

33
JARED

Jared sat in the silent darkness and waited. Kassidy had been gone for a good half hour now. At one point he thought he'd heard her voice, but there had been nothing since, and he wondered if he'd only imagined it. Had she found Chloe? What about the others? He'd flicked his headlamp on several times – when he just couldn't take the silent blackness any longer – and looked at the same limestone walls and dusty floor in the sudden blinding light, then switched it off and leaned back against the rock.

His knee still throbbed with pain, and now his back and ass were starting to hurt from sitting on the hard floor so long. He tried lying on his side, but that seemed to place more pressure on his knee. At one point he stretched out flat, and that relieved the pain in his back but wriggling around trying to adjust his shoulders to the rocky floor had wrenched his leg and given him a new stab of pain in his knee. He ended up sitting again, his back against the wall.

He still couldn't believe what Kassidy had told him. Things truly were over with her. His stomach burned with anger when he thought of their conversation in the car, and then the way she had clung to him since they'd arrived at the cave. And her confession about Luke, and how saying it was over was supposed to make Jared just forgive her for what had happened. She said she hadn't known what she wanted back in the summer, but she still didn't seem to know. He couldn't take that, all that back and forth. She was toying with his emotions like a cat with a piece of string. When they got out of here, he was calling it quits.

He had no idea what to say to Luke. Part of him wanted to bash the fucker's face in. And yet, knowing Luke as he did, he knew one night with Kassidy had probably meant nothing to him. Luke seemed to keep emotions and sex completely separate. It was this ability that had kept him dogging Chloe all this time, even though she had only just today let him hold her hand. But still. Kassidy wouldn't have made a move like that on her own. She would have needed some encouragement. He wondered when it had happened. And where. The mental image of the two of them together made him break out into a cold sweat.

He rubbed a fist against his forehead. Dammit, he had to stop thinking about it. If he kept on like this the thoughts would drive him crazy. Just get through today, get the fuck out of this cave, and then he didn't have to see her again. And maybe later in the week he might look at getting into another apartment and getting away from Luke. There were some nicer places a little farther from campus. Cheaper, too. His parents would love that.

His stomach rumbled, and he realized he hadn't eaten anything since the bag of Combos in the car. He still had a Three Musketeers in his backpack. He reached for it and felt something brush his fingers. What the *fuck?*

He fumbled with the lamp and switched it on. There was nothing there. It must have been his imagination. The dark and the silence must be getting to him. Had to be. He dug out the candy bar and turned off the light, then tore off the wrapper and took a bite.

As he sat chewing, he heard something off to his right. Something moving. He froze, then turned the headlamp back on. Nothing but the same gray rock formations. "Kassidy? Is that you?" Nothing. "Chloe?"

After a minute or so, he switched the light back off and took another bite of the candy. Again he wondered if Kassidy had found Chloe. What if she had gotten lost? Maybe that was why she hadn't come back yet. But if it had been Chloe they had heard calling for help, where were Brandon and Luke?

For the first time, panic gnawed at his gut. What if something had happened to *all* of them? What if there had been another tunnel collapse somewhere else? What if they were all lying hurt somewhere? What was he going to do, stuck here with no way to get to them and no way to call for help?

"Kassidy! Where are you?" His voice rang back to him, flat and hollow. He strained to listen for anything – a voice, a whimper – something to let him know they had heard him. There was nothing.

"Luke! Brandon!"

Silence.

Something was wrong. Kassidy at least should have been back by now. Even if Chloe was lying hurt somewhere, Kassidy would have come back to tell him. Chloe's voice hadn't sounded that far away. Just past the slope where she and the others had disappeared a couple of hours ago.

"*Kassidy!*"

He slumped back against the cave wall. His heart pounded in his chest and he took a deep breath. He didn't want a panic attack like Kassidy had earlier.

Maybe Luke and Brandon had found the way out. Maybe they were outside and had called 911. Maybe they were waiting for help to arrive so they could bring them back down here to get him. Maybe Chloe had gotten hurt and they had left her behind and that's why she had been calling out.

But where was Kassidy?

He heard the sound of movement again. A slow, whispery sound, barely audible. A sound like. . . *slithering.*

His fingers found the light switch and flipped it on. He barely noticed the warmth as his bladder let go and the urine puddled around him. Barely realized he was screaming.

Snakes. They were everywhere. Dozens of them. Draped over rocks. Tangled among his and Kassidy's backpacks. Moving across the cave floor. Moving toward him. The light glinted in their black eyes and their pink forked tongues flicked the air, feeling his warmth.

His arm shot out and shoved the backpacks away from him and the snakes twisting on top went flying away into the darkness.

One had glided close to the heel of his shoe. The tongue slipped from its mouth and tasted the air. It coiled its body and lifted its head, looking at him. Jared kicked at it, knocking it away in a cloud of dust.

Others appeared at the edge of the light, and he realized he had been wrong. There weren't dozens. There were *hundreds*. They kept emerging from the shadows, joining the shimmering, slithering mass that crept ever closer. How long had they been grouping, waiting to move in on him? How had so many gathered so quickly? If only he had something – a torch or a small fire to keep them back. Fleetingly, he remembered Kyle's backpack and the stash of flares, but he recalled Luke and the others taking it with them.

Something cold and smooth wriggled across the fingers on his right hand. He jerked back and saw two grayish bodies curling and twisting together, all four of their eyes locked on his. Mustering every ounce of strength within him, he grabbed hold of the squirming mass to toss it away. One of the things struck at him, catching its fangs in the fabric of his sleeve and hanging in midair. It worked its jaws savagely, struggling to get through to his skin. Both of the snakes tightened around his wrist. He shook his arm, trying to loosen them, trying to get them off, but they coiled tighter.

There was weight on his injured leg. A larger serpent, thick as Jared's forearm, rested on his thigh. Its triangular head slid closer to Jared's urine-soaked crotch. He moved to kick it off, but the snake was too heavy and pain stabbed his knee.

Needle-like jabs told him the snakes on his arm had forced their fangs through the sleeve. His hand shot out reflexively, but they held fast.

With his other hand he managed to dislodge the larger snake from his lap and pull at the ones coiled around his arm, but they tightened and struck again.

If he could just get to his feet. If he could just get out of the middle of them he could head in the direction Kassidy and the others had gone. He could get away.

With his good leg he braced his back against the wall and using his left hand pushed himself up. The snakes still clung to his right arm, and he noticed with a mixture of fear and fascination that it had gone numb.

By the time he struggled to his feet, his knee screaming at him the whole way, the snakes had surrounded him. They already covered the area where seconds before his legs had stretched. There was no way he could make his way through them on his bad knee without falling. None.

A wail grew out of the silence and he realized it was coming from his own mouth. Tears coursed down his face. He was going to die here. He had no idea what kinds of snakes these were, but he'd been bitten, and he couldn't feel his arm and the numbness had already spread to his shoulder. Luke and Kassidy and Brandon and Chloe had disappeared. He was alone.

The headlamp sputtered and faded out, leaving him in a void of complete darkness.

He sank down, already feeling the slithering mass creeping up his legs and back and praying for unconsciousness to take over before he felt them on his face.

It didn't.

34

LUKE

For one blinding moment, Luke thought he had taken a wrong turn. They had woven their way back through the amphitheater, past the rock formations with their crude signs, and down into the large corridor lined with columns and stalagmites he remembered leaving just a couple of hours before. But Kassidy and Jared were gone. "This is the right place, isn't it?"

"Of course it is," Brandon said. "There's their backpacks."

"Maybe Kassidy helped him go take a leak," Luke said.

Chloe cupped her hands around her mouth. "Kassidy! Jared!"

Only silence answered them.

"Why would they just go off like that?" Luke said.

"Maybe they thought we weren't coming back," Brandon said.

Luke blew out a breath. "That's fucking ridiculous.

We've only been gone a couple of hours."

"And where would they go?" Chloe said. "Jared could barely walk. Surely they wouldn't have just struck out on their own."

"Maybe they tried to follow us," Brandon said. "Maybe they got lost."

"Oh, this is crazy," Chloe said. "Kassidy! Where are you? Jared!"

They all stood silent for a moment, listening.

"Look around," Brandon said. "Maybe they left a note or something."

Luke prodded the backpacks with the toe of his shoe. The contents of Jared's had spilled out. Burst water bottles and a crushed bag of Fritos lay nearby. "Something's wrong, guys," Luke said. "Even if they had gone off searching for us, they wouldn't have left both their packs."

"You're right," Chloe said. She crouched close to a damp area near the cave wall and wrinkled her nose. "God, it smells like piss here." She started to rise, then stopped, half crouching, staring at something on the limestone. "Luke. What is that?" She pointed to a small dark spot on the wall.

Luke moved closer. His headlamp illuminated the blot. He and Chloe locked glances.

"What is it?" Brandon asked, moving closer.

"I think it's blood," Luke said. A chill rippled through him.

"That means one of them's hurt," Choe said.

Brandon peered down the corridor into the darkness. "Jared! Kassidy!"

Chloe followed Brandon's gaze. "They had to have gone that way. Otherwise we would have met up with them."

Luke nodded. "Let's go."

They headed off down the passage, calling for Jared and Kassidy, stopping occasionally to be quiet and listen for any sign of them.

"I can't imagine them coming this far," Brandon said. "You saw how Kassidy could barely hold him up, even with you helping her, Luke. There's no way she could get him this far by herself."

Luke nodded. It was the very thing he'd been thinking.

"What's that?" Chloe said. She pointed down the passage.

Luke saw it, too. A dot of yellow, just at the edge of their light. But even before they got close enough to make it out, he knew what it was. One of the helmets. Cracked and covered with blood. Luke squatted down and reached out to grab it.

"Don't touch it," Chloe said. Her eyes had welled up, and she looked as if she would be sick.

"I wonder whose it is," Brandon said. "His or hers."

They stared at it for a moment, then Luke rose to his feet. "Well, we know at least one of them came this way."

"Or was brought here by something else," Chloe said. She looked at Luke. "That animal we saw outside. . . Do you think whatever killed it could be in here with us?"

He hadn't thought so a couple of hours ago. But now he didn't know. Something had hurt Jared or Kassidy or maybe both of them. Very badly by the looks of the helmet. And if it was still in here it could be hunting the three of them now. It could be sitting somewhere in the dark watching them for all he knew. He looked around, sweeping his headlamp up and down the corridor.

"Guys, we've got to get out of here," Brandon said. "I say we try to make our way down to the river, just like we planned."

"I'm with Brandon," Chloe said. "Let's find the river and maybe we can follow it back outside."

"The corridor still slopes downward," Brandon said. "If we keep going this direction we're bound to find it."

Luke nodded. "Let's go."

35
CHLOE

Chloe shuffled along between Luke and Brandon. The cave had become one endless corridor of nothing. The same rugged limestone walls. The same dusty floor. The same stalagmites and grottos. She wasn't even looking at anything anymore. It was all blurring together. She just kept walking. Kept putting one foot in front of the other. At one point she pulled out her phone; no signal of course, but she was shocked to see it was going on 5:30. It would be almost dark outside now.

She refused to allow herself to dwell too long on Jared and Kassidy. Earlier she had asked Luke what he thought might have happened to them, and when looked at her without saying anything, she knew what he was thinking. It was what they were all three thinking. She had cried a bit then, more out of fear than anything, and now she just felt numb. It was all simply too much to comprehend.

The conversation in the truck with Kyle floated through her head, and she found herself wondering again about the legends of the cave. Wendigos and spirits and people who had disappeared. Was it possible any of that was true? Had Jared and Kassidy been attacked by something she would have laughed about only this morning? Or was it – more likely – an animal? A bobcat, like Kyle speculated had ripped open the animal outside? Or something larger?

Luke stopped and Chloe bumped into him. "What is it?"

He pointed ahead.

The corridor had opened into a large chamber. Above them, the walls disappeared into the dark nothingness of a seemingly ceilingless shaft. Directly in front of them three passageways veered off in different directions. Two dilapidated wooden benches sat to the side, but there were no markings, no signs, no indication at all of which way to go.

"What do we do now?" Brandon said.

Luke shook his head. "Just choose one, I guess."

Chloe suddenly felt weak. "Guys, I've got to rest a bit. I can't go on right now."

"Agreed," Brandon said. He shrugged out of his backpack and sank onto the floor.

Chloe sat down beside him, pulling off her pack. She was ravenous. She'd had nothing since the pack of trail mix she'd shared with Brandon earlier. She dug out a bag of pretzels and a bottle of water. "Anybody else want something to eat?"

Luke flopped down beside her and pawed through the contents of his own pack. He pulled out a sandwich bag. "Looks like Kyle packed some Cheerios." He opened it and popped one in his mouth. "Honey Nut."

Brandon tore into a pack of peanuts. "I think we should take the passage on the far left," he said, his mouth full. "I figure it heads in the direction of the river."

"What makes you think that?" Luke said. "Any of these could go down to the river. Or none of them."

"It just makes sense," Brandon said. "When we came in, the river was to our left. It's the same logic we used to get to the entrance doors."

"It makes *no* sense," Luke said. "We've curved around in here so much we could be headed in *any* direction. Hell, the river might even be back the way we came."

"I know we curved a bit, but we've basically been going in straight line. It *has* to be down that way."

Chloe blew out a breath. "It makes as much sense as anything else."

Luke looked at her, shaking his head. "I'm telling you, it's a lottery. It's like *Let's Make a Deal.* Door one, two, or three."

"Then maybe we should just draw straws," Chloe said, half-serious. "Or we each take a passage and see where it goes."

"We're not splitting up," Brandon said.

"Relax," Chloe told him, "I was kidding."

Luke crunched his Cheerios. "You know, taking a peek down all those passages may not be a bad idea."

"What if we get lost?" Brandon said. "What if we can't find our way back here?"

"We won't go far," Luke said. "Look." He pulled the coiled rope from his pack. "If nothing else, we leave a rope trail. There's a good fifty feet here. That would get us far enough in to make sure it's a passage we can get through."

"I don't know," Chloe said. "We go fifty feet in and then what? Go fifty feet more? And then by the time we get so far in, we've still lost our way back here."

"So what do you want to do?" Luke said, his voice hard. "Sit here and rot?"

"Maybe we should go back to the entrance doors again. Maybe we should try harder to get through the grate."

"How? You saw that thing. It's solid. It's not coming off the wall."

"We could try. Maybe there's some tools around we didn't see before." She realized tears were rolling down her cheeks again, but she couldn't stop them. "Maybe there's something else we could use to try to pry it out of the rock." She had no idea what she was saying, really. She was just talking. She only knew that she was starting to feel panicky and desperate and she knew she didn't want to die here in the dark. She knew she didn't want to face whatever had happened to Jared and Kassidy. She knew that if she didn't get back out into the sunlight and out of this damp cold she would go insane.

Luke put an arm around her and drew her close, and she let him. And suddenly she was sobbing into his chest and he was holding her while her body heaved with sobs. She held onto him as tightly as she could, as if she could force him to get them out of here, force him to burst through the tons of rock and earth and pull them out. She felt his stubbled cheek brush against her forehead and found comfort in it. Why had she pushed him away for so long? The feel of him next to her, his warmth, was like being wrapped in velvet. She wanted to curl up in him and disappear and never be found. "I'm so tired," she said.

"Let's rest a little," Luke said, pulling away from her. "We've been going all day. We're exhausted."

Behind them, Brandon was lying on his side, his headlamp off. "How long you think these lights with last?"

Luke switched his off. "Hard to say. I can tell mine's dimmer than it was earlier. We've still got the flashlights. And a couple of flares."

Chloe felt a stab of panic. She'd forgotten about running out of light. What if the batteries in their head-lamps and the flashlights died before they found the river? What if they were lost in here in total darkness? There would never be any way for them to get out. Ev-er. Just like the cavers who disappeared. They would never be found.

Apparently, all of those thoughts showed clearly on her face, because Luke reached up and switched off the light on her helmet. "We're gonna get out of here," he said, running his fingers around the curve of her cheek. "We're gonna make it, I promise."

And even though she couldn't see his face, she imagined him smiling.

36

BRANDON

Brandon lay in the silence, listening to Luke's and Chloe's steady breathing. He had slept some, how long he didn't know, but it seemed like hours. His back was stiff and hurting from his fall and from lying on the rock floor, and pain throbbed in his temples. His stomach growled, and he wondered if he could get something out of his pack without waking the others. Better to let them sleep. Especially Chloe.

But his bladder was straining and – oh no, please not now – he also had to take a dump. He had to find some place to relieve himself. Soon.

He reached for his helmet and switched the lamp on, facing it away from the others. In the ambient glow, he could see them lying together. Chloe was nestled with her back against Luke, and his hand draped across her waist. He felt a pang of jealousy – why he didn't know – and looked away.

He perched the helmet atop his head and grabbed his

pack, wondering if he had anything in there he'd be able to clean himself up with. He vaguely remembered a few wrapped hand wipes lying on his desk – remains of take-out from KFC, but he couldn't remember whether he had packed them. He moved out of the chamber and back down the passage from where they had emerged earlier.

A large outcropping hid a smaller corridor they hadn't noticed from the direction they had come. He stepped into it and barely got his pants unfastened before the stream of urine shot out of him, soaking the wall and floor in front of him. His bladder relaxed in blessed relief as the force of the stream died.

He slid his jeans down and hunched over, balancing on his toes. He dug through the pack and found two hand wipes at the very bottom. Only two, but they would have to do, and it was better than nothing. When he was finished, he swiped at himself as best he could, then stood and pulled up his jeans. He hoped the smell wouldn't carry through to the chamber where Luke and Chloe were, but there was not a lot he could do about it.

He had just picked up his backpack when a skittering sound in the back of the tunnel made him freeze. He felt his testicles draw up to his body. At first he thought of the passage collapsing on Kyle, and the soft click of falling pebbles that had preceded it. This was different. This sounded like something alive and moving over the rock. Something that had been in the tunnel with him this whole time.

This had been stupid, coming in here alone. He never should have left Chloe and Luke. Never. Whatever was in the passageway was moving closer, though still far enough away he couldn't see it in the dim light from his helmet. He kept his eyes on the darkness and backed out of the tunnel into the main corridor.

He was just rounding the corner into the chamber when Luke appeared suddenly in front of him, holding a small flashlight. "What the fuck you doing, Brandon?"

Brandon glanced behind him in the blackness. "Something's back there," he said. "I was taking a shit. Something was moving in there."

Luke craned to see behind him. He pulled him into the chamber. "Come on. Chloe's awake and I think it's time we get out of here."

37
LUKE

They shouldered their packs and stared at the three options in front of them. "Which one?" Luke said.

"Let's go with Brandon's choice," Chloe said.

Luke looked at her, then at Brandon. "You still think the one on the left will lead us to the river?"

Brandon nodded. "I do."

Luke decided there wasn't time to argue. As crazy as Brandon's logic sounded, it was as good as any. "Let's go."

He led them into the narrow passageway and down a series of natural steps. The walls here were jagged and tore at their clothes. And though he told himself he wasn't really seeing it, there were scratches in the rock's surface that looked like claw marks. Something had been through here. A bobcat couldn't have made those scratches. This had been something much bigger. A bear maybe.

Brandon and Chloe said nothing behind him, and he

hoped they hadn't noticed. He was worried about Chloe. She had always seemed strong and independent, one of the reasons he'd been attracted to her initially. But this was wearing her down. He could see it. Hell, it was wearing all of them down.

He didn't want to think what might have happened to Kassidy and Jared, but the claw marks on the wall gave him some idea. Something must have attacked them. But if that was the case, why hadn't there been more blood than just a single smear on the rock? He thought of the cracked and bloodied helmet they had found and wondered what could have hit it hard enough to break it. A bear. It had to be. It was the only thing big enough to have done that. But then again, *why so little blood?*

"Luke, slow down," Brandon said behind him.

Luke turned and saw Chloe and Brandon several yards behind. Chloe was struggling to step over the larger rocks through the narrow passage. "Sorry," he said. He let them catch up. "You guys doing all right?"

Chloe nodded, and her red-rimmed eyes threatened to spill tears. "I'm sorry I'm so slow. I'm just so tired."

Luke reached out and squeezed her shoulder. "It's all right. I'll try not to go so fast."

"Can you see anything up ahead?" Brandon asked.

Luke's eyes searched the darkness ahead. The tunnel continued on past the reach of the light. "No. Nothing." He looked back at Chloe and Brandon. "Let's keep moving."

They continued on down through the passage. It was endless and mind-numbingly repetitive. Luke forced his feet to keep going. One more step. Then another and another. He fought the rising panic in his belly. What if they never found the river? What if the tunnel was just leading them farther and farther away from it? What if they were so deep into the cave they could never find their way back, even to the barred entrance?

Just as these thoughts were flooding his mind, the passage sloped upward and they ascended another series of natural steps. The tunnel opened up into a large chamber.

"No," he said as they emerged into the expansive space. "No! Fuck no!"

They were back in the shaft where they had started. The old wooden benches were at the side, and the other two passageways veered off into the darkness.

38

BRANDON

Brandon took off his helmet and swiped a hand through his sweaty hair. "I don't believe this."

"The tunnel must have circled completely around," Chloe said. Tears were coursing down her cheeks.

Luke blew out a breath. "God*dammit!*" He whirled and stared hard at Brandon. "See where your fucking logic got us? I knew we shouldn't have listened to you. I fucking *knew it!*"

Brandon's stomach was on fire. He could feel his eyes stinging and knew he was about to cry. He blinked back the tears. "I'm sorry," he said.

Luke ripped off his helmet and took a step toward him. "*Sorry?* That was all for nothing. For fucking *nothing!*"

"I didn't see you coming up with any better suggestions," Brandon said, trying hard to keep the tremor out of his voice.

"Stop it!" Chloe cried. She looked from one to the

other. "Please. This isn't solving anything." Her wet face glistened in the glow of their lamps. She put a hand on Luke's shoulder. "We can't freak out on each other. It wasn't Brandon's fault."

Luke tore away from her. "Are you kidding me? This whole fucking mess is Brandon's fault. It was his stupid idea to come to this cave in the first place." He paced back and forth, his hands on his head.

"No one made you come with us," Brandon said. "You were all for it Friday night."

"Yeah, and I was half-drunk, too," Luke said.

Chloe held up her hands. "Guys! Please stop." She wiped her eyes on her dusty sleeve. "Look, let's go back toward the entrance again. There's *got* to be some way through those doors. There's got to be some way to get that grate out of the way."

Luke blew out a breath. "Yeah," he said. "I agree with you."

"Maybe we could find something in that amphitheater," Brandon said. Some tools or something."

"There's got to be something we can use," Chloe said.

Luke perched his helmet back on his head. "Let's go." He headed for the main corridor and glanced back at them. "Come on, girls."

Brandon followed Chloe out of the chamber. He thought again of the noises he had heard earlier in the small passage, the sounds of something creeping closer. He didn't want to come face to face with whatever had been lurking around in there. Whatever might have lured away Jared and Kassidy. Or dragged them away. The image of the bloody helmet flashed through his mind, and his whole body shuddered. They would have to pass it again. And the spot where they had last been seen.

"Should we try to call for Kassidy and Jared?" Chloe asked, and Brandon knew she had been thinking the same thing.

"I don't know," Luke said. "If there's something else in here with us, I don't know that we should call attention to ourselves."

"I agree," Brandon said, surprising himself. "If we can get out of here, if we can get help, the authorities can send in a search party."

"Search party never found those other cavers," Chloe said, and they continued up the passage in silence.

Chloe was right, and Brandon tried hard to push that fact from his mind. Had something actually attacked those cavers? For that matter, had something actually attacked Jared and Kassidy? Or had they all just become lost? But if so, what was the explanation for the bloody helmet? He wasn't sure he wanted to know the answer to any of those questions. Just keep going forward. Just keep moving. Get to the entrance. They would figure some way out. They had to. He was not going to die in this cave.

Chloe had checked her phone and announced it was a little after nine. But time had lost all meaning here in the dark. He knew he should be hungry, but the thought of food nauseated him. Earlier he had finished a bottle of water, and now he had only one left. If they ended up being stranded down here for days, that would be a problem. They would die without water. All those times he had watched Bear Grylls on TV and laughed at him drinking his own urine, he'd never suspected it might one day be a reality.

He wondered if anyone knew he was missing yet, and he doubted it. It was sometimes a week or more between conversations with his mother, and since he had just talked with her yesterday it didn't seem likely she would try to get in touch with him this soon. And there was no dorm roommate to wonder about him, and most of the guys on his floor would be used to him staying in his room and keeping to himself. But surely someone in the financial aid office would notice when he failed to show up for work tomorrow. Betty, his supervisor, would know something was wrong. He'd never missed a day without calling in. And when she couldn't reach his cell she'd try to call his mother. He was sure Chloe and Luke would be in similar circumstances. And even Jared and Kassidy.

But Kyle's family would be searching, too, and that gave him a spark of hope. Kyle hadn't been ignorant about things like the rest of them. As experienced and cautious as he was, he would have made sure someone knew where they were going. And someone would come looking. Maybe sooner than later. Someone would find the cars. Someone would know they were in the cave.

"Careful," Luke said, "it's getting narrow through here."

"I don't remember this," Chloe said. "Are you sure we came the right way?"

"Has to be," Luke said. "There haven't been any tunnels leading off from this one. And we passed that godawful stink Brandon made."

"Shouldn't we have passed the spot where we left Jared and Kassidy by now? I've been watching for their backpacks."

"And the helmet," Brandon said. "We haven't seen the helmet."

"We just haven't got there yet," Luke said. "Jesus, calm down, you two."

"I'm telling you, we didn't come this way," Chloe said. "We went past formations and stalagmites. There's none of that here."

"This is the only way we could have come," Luke said.

"I don't remember any of this," Chloe said. "The way we came wasn't this narrow."

Luke stopped and turned to face them. "It has to be this way. It's the only thing that makes sense."

"Nothing makes sense in here," Chloe said. "Does it make sense that Jared and Kassidy would have wandered off by themselves? Does it make sense that if something attacked them there would be more than just one spot of blood on the rocks?"

"Or one bloody helmet?" Brandon said.

Luke glared at him. "Shut up about the fucking helmet." He wiped his face on his sleeve and looked at Chloe. "What do you want to do? Turn back?"

"I just think we took a wrong turn somewhere," she said. "If we just go back and retrace our steps – "

Luke's eyes narrowed. "You two do whatever the fuck you want." He turned and headed down the passage. "I'm going this way."

Brandon looked at Chloe. "We've got to stick together. It's the only hope we've got of getting out of here."

She nodded, then silently followed Luke. She looked as if she would start crying again, and Brandon didn't know it he could take any more of that. God, he was tired. They were all tired. Tired and snapping at each other. If they could just get back to the entrance, maybe they could rest a while before they tried to free the grate. It seemed like hours since they had napped. Days since they had seen Jared and Kassidy. A month since they had crawled in here.

"Watch out," Luke said. "We're going to have climb over some big rocks here."

Chloe shot Brandon a glance, and he tried to ignore the fear in her eyes. He knew now they were going the wrong way. They hadn't come over any big rocks. They hadn't come through any narrow passages. Luke had no idea where they were headed, and they were letting him lead them into God-knew-what.

Luke put out a hand to help Chloe up, and Brandon noticed he couldn't meet her eyes. Luke knew. He knew they were lost. The expression on his face said it all.

"There had to be something we missed back there," Brandon said. He pulled himself over the boulders and found himself standing in a narrow passage with Chloe and Luke.

"There was no other way to go," Luke said. "Did you see any other corridors branching off?"

Brandon blew out a breath. "No." He knew Luke was right. There had been no choice but to keep moving forward.

Luke took off his helmet and swiped his face across his sleeve. "Look, I know we didn't come this way, but it's the only way back. It has to be." He put the helmet back on and started moving down the passage.

Brandon nodded his head in Luke's direction.

"Come on," he said to Chloe.

They had followed Luke only a few hundred yards when the tunnel opened up. Luke stopped and gazed around him. "Fuck," he whispered. "Oh, fuck this isn't happening."

Brandon and Chloe emerged and fear gripped the base of Brandon's spine. "It's not real," he said. "It can't be real."

They were back in the chamber where they had started.

39

LUKE

Luke stared in disbelief. It was the same place, all right. They had emerged from the middle passage, and the wooden benches and the opening to the main corridor – the corridor they had headed down just an hour before – was across from them.

"How is that *possible*?" Brandon said.

Chloe was shaking her head as tears rolled down her face. "There something wrong with this place," she said. "Something's fucking with us. This can't be happening." She looked at Luke and her eyes were bloodshot and pleading. "We're gonna die in here," she said, her voice barely a whisper. "We're never getting out of here."

Luke took her by the shoulders and looked into her eyes. "We're gonna make it," he said. "Trust me."

She put her head against his chest and sobbed. "I'm so scared," she said.

He held her tight. "I know. We all are."

Brandon had sunk to the floor. "Let's rest," he said. "Then we'll figure out our next move."

"Good idea," Luke said. He helped Chloe out of her backpack. She was shivering. "You cold?"

"I'm freezing," she said. "I haven't been warm since we got in this place."

Luke glanced at the old benches. "Brandon, help me bust up one of those benches and we'll build a little fire."

"You sure that's wise?" Brandon said. "You don't think we'll get carbon monoxide poisoning or anything do you?"

Luke looked up into the nothingness above them. "This dome looks so high, we should be all right. We won't make it very big."

The bench was surprisingly sturdy, but by wedging it at an angle against the cave wall, the two of them managed to break the slats of the back into several pieces using their feet. Brandon arranged them on the floor while Luke dug through the backpack. "I've heard of fires in caves causing the rock to collapse," Brandon said.

Luke pulled out the plastic box of matches. "We'll be fine, Brandon," Luke said. "It's just gonna be a small fire. Just enough to get warm and give us a little light. We need to conserve the batteries in our head-lamps."

But after using three matches, Luke could not get the wood to catch. It was either damp or too hard.

"What about using a flare?" Brandon said.

Luke shrugged. "We can try it."

Chloe shook her head. "Not a good idea, guys. The smoke from those things is toxic."

"What about the one Kyle lit?" Luke said.

"We were in a bigger space," Chloe said. She nodded at the pack. "Didn't you say there was a candle in Kyle's pack? You took it, didn't you?"

"What good's a candle gonna do?" Luke said.

"It's better than nothing," Chloe said. "It'll at least put off a little heat. I've always heard a candle would keep you from freezing to death if you were stranded in the cold in a car."

Luke shook his head. Whatever. He felt in the pack until his fingers closed around the candle. He set it upright on the cave floor and lit it with one of the remaining matches. Instantly the chamber was filled with a golden flicker.

He leaned back and gazed upwards. The ceiling of the dome couldn't be seen. It appeared endless.

Chloe huddled over the flame, holding out her hands to the warmth. Luke reached over and clicked off her headlamp and she smiled up at him. "I'm so tired," she said.

"I know, babe."

Brandon hulked beside her, staring into the light. "I think Chloe's right," he said. "I think there's something wrong with this place."

Luke took a sip of tepid water, then recapped his bottle. "There's no way we circled back," he said. "We went out of here the same way we came in the first time."

Chloe looked at him. "It's like the cave is. . . *changing*."

He opened his mouth to tell her that was impossible, but then stopped himself. She was right. They might have gone around a bend or two, but even if they had taken a wrong turn it would have been impossible for them to stumble back into this chamber twice. Unless the corridor had *twisted* somehow. But caves didn't move around. That didn't make sense. They were solid. Unyielding.

Brandon stretched out on his side. "I wonder if that's what happened to Jared and Kassidy. The cave changed on them, and they couldn't find their way back."

"Then how do you explain the blood?" Luke said. He took a seat in front of the candle and looked at Chloe. "What was that thing you were telling us about on the way down here? A wendigo?"

Chloe nodded. "If you believe those stories." She sighed. "But even if there was such a creature, and even if it attacked Jared and Kassidy, that doesn't explain what's happening to us. A wendigo can't alter its surroundings." She looked around. "This is more like legends I've heard about caves being portals into other dimensions, tears in the fabric of time and space."

Luke blew out a breath. He didn't know what to say to that. He didn't believe in that kind of nonsense, didn't believe in anything he couldn't see or touch. But just because he didn't believe it couldn't change what they had experienced. Something was keeping them here. Something was toying with them. It didn't take a believer in pseudo-scientific babble to understand that.

They sat in silence for a while until Brandon began to snore. Chloe stretched out and soon she, too, was out. Just as well. If anyone needed to rest it was Chloe. The stress had worn her down, and Luke had seen that tough, independent exterior of hers break. It melted his heart. He had been attracted first to her strength, but now that she was vulnerable he felt something he'd never experienced before. He watched her sleep, her eyelids fluttering slightly, and he sensed an aching desire to protect her. He would get her out of here. He would get her back outside if he died trying.

He arched his back and stretched, and he had just rolled onto his side when he thought he heard music. Tinny and far away. Was he hearing things?

He sat up and listened. It came again, insistent and repeating. The Apple marimba tone. A cell phone. And if it was ringing, that meant it was getting a signal.

He stood and cocked his ear. Where was it coming from?

The ringtone came again. He followed the sound. It was coming from the third passage. He glanced back at Brandon and Chloe. They continued to sleep in the flickering glow of the candle.

Luke pulled the flashlight from his pocket and flicked it on. The cell phone was still ringing. He entered the tunnel. The sound was louder here, but he still couldn't locate the source. The path wound around a bend and widened out. Steel handrails curved around a steep dropoff, and a wooden painted sign read *The Bottomless Pit*. This had been the way all along. The tour route continued through this passage, and it probably led directly to the river.

The light brushed something shiny and pink in the dust. An iPhone. Kassidy's. He recognized the case. The display read "Jared." It rang again, and he leaped to grab it. "Hello?"

"Luke!" It was Kassidy. She was crying.

"Kassidy! Where are you? Is Jared with you?"

"Oh, Luke!" she sobbed.

"What happened? Are you hurt?"

Kassidy continued to cry. "Luke, why did you hurt me?"

"What?"

"All I ever wanted was to love you."

"Kassidy – "

"You just wanted to fuck me. You just wanted me to spread my legs for you."

Luke's face burned. "Kassidy, stop it. Where are you? Can you call for help?"

"Jared knows, Luke. Jared knows and he's coming after you. He's going to kill you for what you did."

Luke's stomach clenched with fear. Something wasn't right. "Stop talking and listen to me. Where are you? Are you still in the cave? Kassidy!"

But she was gone, and he was talking to a dead line. He looked at the screen. There was no signal.

A shape loomed up out of the darkness, something covered with brown fur. Thin arms stretched from a hairy torso with hands that ended in yellow extended claws. Unable to stop himself, Luke raised the light to the thing's face, illuminating the long snout and black eyes. It opened its mouth, and saliva dripped from the stained, fang-like teeth. It moved toward him.

The metal handrail pressed against the small of Luke's back. There was no place to go. His arms and legs were completely numb with fear.

The creature lashed out with a hairy hand and razor-like claws sliced through Luke's cheek. He jumped back reflexively and too late remembered the drop-off behind the handrail. *The Bottomless Pit.* The rail caught him just below the waist and he went tumbling backwards into the dark, flying into the nothingness below.

40

CHLOE

Chloe stirred and stretched. It was the first time she hadn't been cold since they had come into the cave. She knew it had to be psychological; the heat from the small candle wasn't nearly enough to keep her warm. She opened her eyes and saw Brandon at her feet. He was lightly snoring. She wondered how things would be between them when they finally got out of here. Even though Brandon was gay, she couldn't imagine ever being closer to another human being in her life. They were soul mates, and somehow in some sick twisted way, they were destined to be together. Maybe not as lovers, but companions nonetheless.

She reached out for Luke, but her hand felt nothing but the cave floor. She raised up. He was gone.

She had just started to call out to him when he appeared in one of the passageways. He put a finger to his lips and came toward her. "Where did you go?" she whispered.

He lay down beside her and wrapped his muscular arms around her, pulling her back down to the floor. "Don't talk," he said. He put his hand to her cheek and kissed her on the lips. She looked behind her, at Brandon lying in the flickering candlelight. "It's okay," Luke said. "He's asleep."

He kissed her again, and she kissed him back, tasting the salty sweat on his lips, feeling the stubble of his beard against her cheek. His hand caught the zipper of her hoodie and tugged it down, then meandered under her t-shirt and lightly traced over her breast through her bra. Her heart hammered within her. She felt the hard muscles of his chest through his shirt, moved her fingers lower and brushed something harder between his legs. Pleasure and desire coursed through her. She was going to do this. Even here in this godforsaken cave with Brandon lying not two feet away and the chance they might never see daylight again. She wanted him. More than anything. She pulled back and looked at him, still tasting him on her lips, and his eyes met hers. His eyes were so dark and glistening with passion. With need. She kissed him again and then stopped.

She pulled away and stared into his eyes. Luke's eyes were green, not dark. This was wrong. Something was wrong. "No," she said, pushing him away.

"What?"

She pushed harder, but he held her like a vice. "No!"

He grinned at her, and his tongue, bright red and forked, snaked through his lips.

She screamed, beating at him with her fists. "Brandon!"

She was vaguely aware of Brandon on his feet behind her. "What the hell are you doing, Luke?" he said.

"Get him off me!"

Brandon grabbed Luke and pulled him loose from Chloe, and the two of them tumbled to the ground away from her.

Luke rose to his feet. Brandon still lay on the cave floor in a daze. "What the hell's wrong with you?" Brandon said.

Chloe rushed to him. "That's not Luke," she said.

As they watched in horror, the thing that was not Luke shook violently. Its head cracked open, ripping the face down the middle like a mask in a shower of blood. Something was emerging from inside, something with a wolf-like snout.

Brandon grabbed one of the broken bench slats from the floor and held it in front of him like a sword. He got to his feet and shoved Chloe behind him. "Keep back."

The thing continued its metamorphosis. The clothes fell away revealing a bony pale body covered with tufts of black hair. It opened its mouth and roared, a sound more human than animal. Its black eyes were locked on them.

Brandon rushed at it, plunging the slat into its chest. It howled and took a step back, pawing at the stake buried between its ribs. With one last glance at them, it fled through the opening back into the main corridor of the cave, its cries echoing back into the chamber.

Brandon looked at the bloody mess before them, then glanced at Chloe. "Let's get the fuck out of here."

41
BRANDON

"What the hell was that?" Chloe cried, strapping on her pack.

"I don't know," Brandon said, dousing the candle with a pinch of his fingers and tossing it into his backpack. As an afterthought, he decided to take what little was in his own pack and throw it into Luke's. Better to take everything than leave something important behind.

"You think that thing might have attacked Kassidy and Jared?"

Brandon glanced back at corridor where the creature had disappeared and shouldered Luke's pack. "I don't know, Chloe."

"And what's happened to Luke? That wasn't really him, was it?" Her eyes were glistening in the firelight, and her bottom lip quivered. He could see it was taking everything within her to not cry again. "That thing was touching me! It was *touching me!*"

He put a hand on her shoulder. "Don't freak out on

me. Right now we just need to get away from here."

Chloe looked at the three passageways ahead of them. She pointed to the one at the far right. "That's the only one we haven't been in."

Brandon looked at her and flicked on his headlamp. "Let's go." He grabbed Chloe's hand and pulled her into the tunnel.

The passage quickly widened out to a flat area ringed with steel handrails. A wooden sign, similar to the others they had seen before, read *The Bottomless Pit*. "We must be on the right track," Chloe said. "I'm sure the tour went this way."

Brandon glanced behind them into the darkness. He was afraid the thing he'd fought off would show itself any moment. "Come on."

The trail sloped downward and jagged rock walls pressed in on them once again. The river had to be down this way, it just had to. A dark dread clawed at his belly. What if he was wrong? What they never found the river? What if they ended up back in the chamber again? Or worse, what if they found the river but still couldn't find the way out of the cave? Their headlamps had grown considerably dimmer; how much longer would they hold out? He reached for his pocket and felt the flashlight Kyle had given him outside a hundred years ago. What would they do if they used up all their light sources? He tried to push the thoughts from his mind and concentrate on moving through the passage, focus on one step at a time, on the play of the lamplight as it rippled across the walls, on the deafening silence as he strained his ears for any sound of the creature.

Behind him, Chloe was crying again. "They're all

dead, aren't they? Kassidy and Jared. Luke."

He stopped and turned to her. "We don't know that. Maybe they got out."

"Luke wouldn't have left us!" she cried. "And you saw that thing! It was pretending to be him. And it knew! Somehow it knew about him and me!" She pressed her hands to her mouth and sobbed. "Oh, Brandon, I'm scared. I'm really scared!" She clung to him and he wrapped his arms around her. Her body convulsed with sobs. "What if it comes back? What if it comes back!"

He stepped away from her and took her by the shoulders. "Stop it. We've got to keep moving. We're gonna get out of here, but you're going to have to stay calm. We can do this. All right?"

She nodded and wiped the tears off her cheek with the back of her hand. "I'm sorry."

"Don't be sorry. I need you to be strong for me." He looked into her eyes. "Remember the dude in the parking lot last year?"

Her eyes widened, and he knew he'd struck a nerve. "That was different," she said. "That was a whacked-out man. This. . . thing. We don't know what it is."

"But you got away from that guy," Brandon told her. "And do you know why? Because you used your head and didn't panic. This is the same thing. We've got to use our heads if we want to get out of here." He took her hand. "Come on, let's get moving."

She hid her face in her hands. "Brandon, I'm so tired. I can't go on much longer."

"I know. But we've got to keep going. We don't know if or when that thing might show up again."

He led her on down the passage, through a narrow

section marked *Fat Man's Squeeze*, and into a larger corridor lined with squat, fat columns. The floor evened out here, but just as quickly as the space had opened up, the trail ended abruptly at the edge of a precipice. A narrow rope bridge spanned the gulf. Many of its ancient floorboards were cracked or missing, and the interlaced cords forming the sides were dusty and frayed.

He wondered fleetingly whether the bridge would support them, wondered when the last person had crossed it. He had just opened his mouth to share these feelings with Chloe when the ear-splitting howl of the creature echoed through the chamber. It was behind them somewhere in the passage, and not too far away by the sound of it.

"We're going to have to cross here," he said.

Chloe looked at him, her eyes wide and frightened. "Are you crazy? I'm not setting foot on that."

"We've got no choice," he said. "That thing's right behind us."

Chloe shook her head. "Brandon, I can't do it! I can't!"

The howl came again, louder this time.

Brandon took her face in his hands and peered into her eyes. "Chloe, you've got to. We've got to get across here."

Chloe whimpered and shot a glance at the rope bridge. "Brandon – "

"Do you want to end up like Luke?"

She shook her head, tears spilling down her cheeks.

"Then you've got to do this. It's our only chance."

She stared at the tattered bridge in front of them, then glanced back at him. Again the howling penetrated the silence. She closed her eyes and bit her lips. Her hands squeezed his.

"I want you to go first," he told her.

Her eyes bulged. "Why me?"

"Because that thing is close, and if only one of us has time to get across here, I want it to be you."

She looked up at him, and he expected her to protest, but she merely nodded her head. She leaned up on her tiptoes and kissed his cheek, then turned and grabbed hold of the ropes.

42

CHLOE

Chloe took a deep breath, trying to ignore how it rattled in her chest, and set her foot on the first dusty plank. It creaked in protest.

"Try to stay as close to the edge as possible," Brandon said behind her. "Hold tight to the rope."

"Don't worry," she said.

Across the chasm, the bridge stretched into the darkness. It was only about fifty feet. She could do this. She could. Below was infinite blackness. How far down the abyss extended she couldn't tell. Nor did she want to know.

"Don't look down," Brandon said. "Just keep going."

Her heart was pounding like a hammer, and she could feel her pulse in her hands where she gripped the rope. Just fifty steps. She blew out a breath.

She stepped onto the next plank with her right foot and the bridge swayed with the movement. Fighting the urge to vomit, she forced her left foot to follow. Forty-eight steps. Another two steps. Forty-six. She was doing it. She continued to inch forward, ignoring the groaning of the planks.

"You're doing good," Brandon said. "Keep going."

"I don't hear that thing anymore," Chloe said, watching as her hands inched their way over the dust-coated rope.

"Don't think about it," he said. "You just concentrate on getting across."

Beside her right foot, one of the wooden planks had splintered away like a rotten tooth. She eased over the empty space and stepped onto the next plank. Sweat was trickling down her forehead, stinging her eyes, but she didn't dare let go of the rope to wipe her face. She brought her left foot alongside her right, wishing there was some way to keep from pressing her full weight onto the boards. A dull ache throbbed behind her eyes. Her hands gripped the rope so tightly that her fingers were numb.

"You're halfway there," Brandon said.

Halfway. Just twenty-five more steps. She was doing it! She was –

Her right foot slipped between two of the planks and thrust into nothingness. She was going to fall through. Her breath left her. Holding tight to the rope with both hands and using her left leg as leverage, she tugged her right foot back between the planks and felt a needle-sharp sting as a splinter pricked her ankle just above her shoe. She managed to pull loose and dropped her head to the rope between her hands. For a moment, her heart had stopped, and now she held tight as she began to shake.

"You okay?" Brandon called.

Chloe clenched her eyes closed and swallowed hard, willing the vertigo away. She concentrated on keeping her knees from buckling. "I'm all right."

"You've almost made it, Chloe."

She opened her eyes and could see the path continuing on the other side. It couldn't be more than ten feet away. Ten fucking feet. She could do it.

She took a deep determined breath and managed to make the last few steps without stopping. As soon as her feet hit the limestone, she collapsed in a heap, shaking and nauseated.

"Good job," Brandon said. "I'm starting over now."

"Be careful," she said, and realized how stupid that sounded.

She watched as he stepped out onto the bridge, gripping the ropes with both hands and easing across the boards. The bridge groaned considerably more under Brandon's massive frame, and Chloe tensed as his shoes settled on one dry-rotted plank, then another.

A shrieking howl cut the silence. The creature emerged from the darkness across the gorge and sniffed the air with its glistening snout. It grunted and emitted a low rumble from its hairy chest.

Chloe cried out. "Hurry up!"

Brandon took a glance behind him and tried to quicken his pace. But just as he was only a few steps away, the unthinkable happened. With a pinging snap, one of the ropes securing the far side of the bridge gave way, and the floorboards dropped from beneath Brandon's feet. Chloe could only watch as Brandon dangled in the air by one hand that clutched the remaining rope in a death grip. He managed to swing his other hand up and grab hold of the cable, but his legs bicycled help-lessly in the air.

The creature shifted back and forth on its doglike back feet. It lifted its head and howled with rage, a sound that nearly split Chloe's skull in two. "Come on!" she screamed at Brandon.

Brandon's face was blood red and glistening with sweat. He glanced at Chloe and his eyes were wide and terrified. His hands inched along the rope – agonizing-ly slowly. He was grunting with every breath, and Chloe knew it was taking every ounce of strength he had left to hang on. His hands edged closer toward her. "You can do it, Brandon," she whispered, and she felt as though she were talking more to herself than to him.

"I can't hold on much longer," he said between gasps. "I can't feel my fingers."

"You're almost here. You can do it! You can!"

The creature across the gorge watched them intently, pacing back and forth, growling and snarling.

Brandon was within inches of the ledge. The toes of his shoes scuffed the wall, sending a clattering of loose rock into the blackness below. One hand managed to reach out to the ledge and Chloe grabbed it, pulling him with everything she had within her. He reached over with his other hand, knocking the helmet off his head. The light spun madly as it descended into the abyss, then winked out as it hit the bottom with a thunk. With Chloe pulling one arm, his other hand grasping for a hold and his shoes clambering up the rocky surface, Brandon managed to crawl onto the ledge and collapse beside Chloe, his chest heaving.

Chloe latched onto him, smothering his sweaty face with kisses. "Oh my God, I thought I was going to lose you. I thought you were going to die!"

Brandon clung to her, buried his face in her neck and sobbed.

Across the chasm, the creature howled with rage. They could see it still pacing in the dim light, down on all fours now like a wolf. It gave them one last glance with its black eyes and disappeared back into the far passageway.

43

BRANDON

Brandon watched the creature scuttle back into the darkness and vaguely wondered if it would somehow circle around and find them again. Deep down he knew that it probably would, that they hadn't seen the last of it. That it would rear its ugly, misshapen head when they least expected it.

Chloe still clung to him. "Are you all right?"

He managed a nod. "I'll live." He wiped his eyes with his shaking fingertips, ashamed that he had cried yet again in front of her. "Sorry I'm such a baby."

Chloe looked at him. "Brandon, you could have been killed. You're not a baby."

"I lost my helmet," he said, and immediately thought of the cracked bloody one they had seen earlier. He felt his pocket and was relieved to find the flashlight was still there. "I've still got the light Kyle gave me."

"I lost mine sometime back," Chloe said. "I have no idea where it is. Save yours and we'll try to get by with the light on my helmet for right now."

"I guess we should get a move on."

"Not unless you're ready."

He looked at her and felt something well up inside him. "I guess I am," he said, climbing to his feet. "I don't want to be still sitting here if that thing comes back."

Chloe reached up and pulled the helmet from her head. "Here. Put this on and lead the way."

"You sure?"

"Yes. You're bigger and stronger. I can follow you."

He reached into his pocket. "Then I want you to take the flashlight."

"No, you keep it."

"Chloe, if something happens. . . if we get separated, you'll need a light."

She seemed to consider this for a moment, consider everything he was implying, and nodded. "All right." She took the flashlight from him and slipped it into her own pocket. "But I'm saving it for now."

"Good idea." He adjusted the straps in the helmet and placed it snugly on top of his head. "Let's go."

Ahead of them stretched another long, narrow corridor. With Chloe following and unable to see precisely where she was stepping in the darkness, their progress was slow. Brandon took careful, measured steps, announcing loose rock or uneven surfaces. She clung to his hand, and he could sense the desperation in her grip, as if letting go of him would mean death. Which, in a way, it might. There were no sounds but the shuffle of their feet on the dusty trail, no smells but their own anxious stench. Brandon could feel every nerve poised and expectant, straining to catch the slightest movement or tiniest echo of anything that could be the thing in here with them.

He was grateful Chloe was with him. He tried to imagine how things would be if he were with one of the others. Jared would be injured and unable to physically make the trek. Kassidy would be panicked and useless. Luke would be trying to take charge without any thought or logic. Only Kyle might have been able to get them through; he had been the only one with experience. But Brandon tried not to think about that now. Kyle for sure was dead. The others, probably so. Chloe was at least sensible and intelligent, and what she lacked in physical ability she was more than making up for in clearheadedness.

"I'm getting really hungry," she said.

Brandon was suddenly aware of his own empty belly. "Yeah, maybe we should stop for a snack."

They unshouldered their packs and sat cross-legged on the path, digging out what was left of the food. Chloe still had one unopened bottle of water and Brandon had half a bag of peanuts plus a package of Combos left from Luke's pack. "Not much left," Chloe said. "I'll take the peanuts and you can have the Combos. You're bigger than me and you'll need more food. We'll split the water."

"We'll split *everything*," Brandon said. "We both need to keep up our strength." He nodded at the water. "Is that the only bottle you've got?"

"The only one that hasn't been opened. I've still got a little bit left in this other bottle."

"Me, too," Brandon said. "Let's save that one. We might need it later."

They ate in silence, trying to pace themselves so they wouldn't scarf down everything in a few bites. Brandon's stomach growled, as if the first taste of food had awoken it, and he was suddenly ravenous. When they were finished, they drained what was left of their waters and sat looking at the empty containers. Now they were down to one bottle for the both of them. Brandon looked at Chloe. They locked glances and he could see in her eyes that she understood the gravity of what that meant. If they had to be in here much longer, if these few hours of being lost turned into days, they could die of dehydration.

"I have to pee," Chloe said, getting to her feet. She took out the flashlight and flicked it on.

"Don't go far," he said.

She aimed the light ahead of her and headed down the corridor. "Talk to me," she said. "I don't like not being able to see you."

"Just look at the light on my helmet," he told her. "Pretend it's a lighthouse and you're on the ocean."

He heard her unzip her jeans and then the quiet trickle of her urine on the path. "When we get out of here, I'm taking you out to dinner," she said. "To that steakhouse on Ninth Street we've been meaning to try."

"Sounds good," he said. "I'm getting the biggest steak they have. And a baked potato."

The jeans zipped up. "And dessert."

"Wonder if they have chocolate cake?"

The light bobbled back toward him. "If they don't, I'll make you one," she said, slipping the flashlight back into her pocket.

"You can cook?"

"Damn straight," she said. "Never get much of a

chance anymore, but when I still lived at home I liked experimenting with recipes. Came up with my own version of chocolate lava cake."

"That sounds awesome," he said, imagining the warm sweet chocolate sliding over his tongue. "You're going to make a good wife someday," he said.

She laughed. "So will you."

He smiled at her, though he knew she probably couldn't see his face very well. "Tell you what, if we're both still single when we're thirty, we'll get married."

"To each other?"

"Why not?"

"A black woman and gay white man?"

"I've seen stranger couples."

She snorted. "Brandon Wright, this cave has made you crazy."

He took her hand. "Come on, let's get going."

44
CHLOE

As difficult as it was following Brandon in the dark, Chloe was thankful to have him leading her, to have his large warm hand in hers. She thought about what he'd said, about their getting married, and though she knew it was a joke, the idea gave her some comfort. The thought of growing old alone terrified her almost as much as the possibility of never getting out this cave. It wasn't about sex – she could have had that many times had she pursued it – it was about companionship. Of having a best friend to go places with, to hang out with. She couldn't have had that with Luke. As much in lust as she was, she knew a relationship with him would be doomed.

Would have been doomed.

Luke was dead, she knew. They were all dead. All of them except her and Brandon.

She squeezed Brandon's hand tighter and concentrated on taking one step at a time. She was not going to allow herself to think about the others. She had to focus on getting out of here, of getting to the river and getting outside. She – *they* – would make it. They had to.

"Careful," Brandon said. "The path is sloping down again. There's a handrail."

"We must still be on the path for the old tour," Chloe said. "That's good, right?"

"I hope so." He started to take another step, then stopped abruptly. "Listen."

"What?"

"*Listen.*"

She stood like a stone, hearing nothing at first but her own thudding heartbeat in her ears. Then, gradually, she could make out something else. The sound of trickling water. "Is that the river?"

"I don't know."

"Which direction is it coming from?"

"I can't tell." He cocked his head. "Somewhere up ahead, I think."

She followed him down the slope, one hand in his and the other gripping the mottled handrail, almost afraid to hope they had found what they had been searching for.

The corridor opened up into a large chamber, much larger than any they had seen so far. The dim light from Brandon's helmet barely penetrated the darkness, and Chloe knew without asking that the headlamp was dying. "Do you want the flashlight?" she asked.

"Not yet. Let's light a flare." He shrugged out of the backpack and dug around until he found it. With a click, a brilliant blue-white light erupted out of the darkness. He tossed the flare toward the center of the chamber and they stared at what lay before them. Chloe's legs lost their strength and she fell to her knees.

A shallow stream ran through the center of the cavern, trickling over the rocks in the streambed. But what held their gaze lay on either side of it. Bones. Thousands and thousands of bones. Piles of bones that rose to mountainous heights in the chamber, past where the pulsating light of the flare could reach. The ones farthest away were gray and splintered, but those closest to them looked fresher, still covered with brownish tags of flesh and sinew. Animal or human, or maybe some mixture of both, it was hard to tell. The smell – putrid and suffocating – was so strong that Chloe wondered why they hadn't noticed it before. She covered her mouth and nose with her hands. "Where are we?"

Brandon's face was white. "I think this is where it lives." He continued to stare at the mounds of bones. "At least, this is where it. . . feeds."

Chloe had just started to turn away, had just opened her mouth to tell Brandon they needed to get the fuck away from here, when something in the far shadows caught her eye. She pulled out the flashlight and shined it toward what looked like bundles of rolled up bed linens. "What is that?"

Together they moved toward the objects, their feet sliding and rolling through loose bone. "Be careful," Brandon said.

Chloe's light caught the first bundle, and before she could stop herself, she screamed.

It was Luke. He was wrapped in something that at first glance looked like thin, sheer fabric. She reached out to touch it and her fingers came back sticky and wet. Behind him lay Kassidy and Jared. All of them wrapped up, all of them gray and unmoving. Their eyes! *Oh, my God their eyes are gone!* Nothing left but mangled black holes where eyes should be.

No. This wasn't happening. This wasn't real. This was some other merciless trick being played on them. Like the shifting cave. Like the thing pretending to be Luke. That was it. It was all in their minds. She wanted to tell Brandon this, to tell him it was some kind of shared hallucination, but nothing would come out of her mouth. She turned and buried her face into his chest.

"Come on," he said. "Let's get to the river and try to get out of here."

They headed back toward the water, their feet unsteady on the shifting pile of bones. Brandon had just helped her back onto the flat surface of the cave floor when a voice came from behind them. "Son?"

They turned.

Brandon's mother stepped out into the light.

45

BRANDON

Brandon stared at his mother as she emerged from the shadows. She was wearing a dark blue suit, the same one she wore to all the bank board meetings. Her blonde hair curled perfectly about her head, and her face was flawless, as if she had just had a makeover. She clasped her immaculately manicured hands in front of her, giving him that look she reserved for when he had committed some grievous sin.

He knew she couldn't be real. He knew this was some sort of vision. The same as when they saw the thing that was not Luke. Still, he couldn't tear his gaze away. "Mom?"

She shook her head. "Oh, Brandon."

Beside him, Chloe clutched his arm. "It's not her. She's not really here."

Logic told him Chloe was right. That his mother was back home in Evansville, Indiana, probably sitting at her desk and turning down some young couple for a house loan. That what he was looking at was some pro-jection, some image that *thing* was stealing from his mind and turning into flesh and bone. "Go away," he said. "You're not real."

She continued to stare at him with that pained ex-pression. "Brandon, your father and I are so disap-pointed in you."

He was aware of Chloe tugging at his arm. "Let's go. Don't listen to her."

"We gave you everything," his mother said. "Did everything loving parents should do. And now you go and do this."

"What?" he said, unable to stop himself from talking to her. To *it*. "What did I do?"

"Brandon, we know. We *know*."

"What? What do you know?"

She shook her head again. "That you're gay. That you're gay and you're going to have to spend eternity in hell."

Chloe's voice became more insistent. "Don't listen, Brandon. It's not real. Let's just get the fuck out of here."

"We thought we raised you better than that," his mother went on. Tears appeared in her eyes and threat-ened to spill down her cheeks. "Can you imagine how you've hurt us? When we found out our son was noth-ing but a filthy cocksucker?"

His fear gave way to anger. "Shut. Up."

"I should have known," she said. "You were always such a sissy about everything. Never wanting to get dirty. Never wanting to play sports with the other boys. Or maybe it was some other kinds of games you wanted to play with them. Was that it? The love that shall not reveal its name? Is that what you wanted? Rolling around with another boy, both of you naked and lusting and wanting to commit the unforgivable sin?"

He covered his ears with his hands. "Shut up! *Shut up!*"

He was vaguely aware of Chloe digging through her backpack, of her muttering curses as she pawed through the contents.

His eyes remained fixed on his mother. "You don't know anything about me," he said. "You never *wanted* to know anything about me. I've been nothing but a big disappointment to you since I was born, haven't I?"

"You've always been a godless child." She wiped her eyes. "And now to think you've gone and turned into a fag. A fag, Brandon! You might just as well as strangled me in my sleep."

Chloe rose up beside him, brandishing a small canister. She flew toward his mother. "Strangle on this, you fucking bitch!" The canister shot forth a stream of red foul-smelling liquid into his mother's eyes.

The thing which was not his mother howled in rage and pain, a sound which could not come from a human. It staggered back, flailing at its eyes. Brandon had just enough time to see what had been his mother's hands had now split, revealing yellowish claws and tufts of black hair.

"Hit it!" Chloe screamed. "Kill it!"

Brandon glanced around for anything he could use as a weapon. Anything at all. He made a desperate grab for large bone sticking up from the pile next to him. It tore away from something buried deep in the mound with sickening resistance.

He took one last look at the thing that was not his

mother, at the face streaked with red liquid and the claws clogged with jagged skin and blood, before he brought the bone down on its skull. It howled and stumbled backward. He swung the bone again, then again, until the perfect blond hair was soiled with blood. It continued moving away from them, hunched over and clutching its head, its mouth open with an unending scream that echoed off the chamber walls and reverberated into Brandon's skull. The pile of bones beneath its feet shifted, and it went tumbling onto its back, his mother's suit skirt riding high above its thighs.

The light shifted, and suddenly Chloe was beside him, wielding the flare like a sword. With one swift movement, she leaped at the creature and plunged the flaming end of the flare into its open mouth.

They watched in horror as the face that moments before had appeared to be Leslie Wright, bank vice president, morphed into that of the wolfish creature they had seen emerge from Luke's skin. The eyes, black and glistening, bulged before exploding into grayish ooze and the flare imbedded in the mouth shot forth flames from the sockets.

Brandon staggered back and fell to the floor, watching what was left of the creature twitch violently and become still. Its fur-covered legs had split through his mother's skin, though they still jutted out from the navy-blue skirt. He repressed a sudden urge to laugh. "Is it dead?"

Chloe knelt beside him. "I don't know. But I don't want to hang around here long enough to find out."

46

CHLOE

For a while they were able to follow the stream by walking along a narrow ledge beside it. The walls of the cave were high and allowed them to stand upright. Brandon led the way again, this time using the flashlight to guide them through the darkness. Chloe's senses remained on high alert; she was terrified any moment she would hear that horrible howl from somewhere behind them, or a scuttle of claws on the rocky surface. Or something splashing toward them in the water.

But none of that happened.

Eventually, the ceiling became lower and they were forced to crawl on their hands and knees. Chloe thought back to crawling through the first tunnel with the others, when she thought it couldn't get worse than that, when she thought the worst she would have to endure would be a couple of broken nails or dirt in her hair, and she felt saddened. It wasn't just that she'd been naïve – hell, they'd *all* been naïve, even Kyle.

She was saddened by the fact that they'd come to a turning point at the end of that tunnel. That they'd had a chance to not go any farther, to head back to the cars and laugh and joke about what a crazy adventure it had been, to bemoan the fact they'd not really seen much of the cave, but what the hell, it had still been fun. And instead they'd pressed on. Part of her blamed Kyle. After all, he was the experienced one. And yes, part of her even blamed Brandon, because it had all been his idea in the first place.

But she knew playing a blame game was pointless. No matter whose fault it was. It had still been all of them that had chosen to go forward. All of them who wanted to keep going. Even Kassidy, who was so hesitant about crawling through that first tunnel, wanted to go deeper. It was nobody's fault. Not really.

She watched Brandon's shape crawling ahead of her. Once or twice his shoes had pinched her fingers against the rock, and she'd made a conscious effort to place a bit more distance from him. As it was, even though he was shining the flashlight straight up at the ceiling and bathing the cavern in dim light, she had no idea really what she was crawling over. All she could do was concentrate on moving forward, just as she had been doing this whole time.

Brandon hadn't spoken a word since they had left the creature smoldering in its lair. She was worried about him. After all, he had just killed his mother – or what looked like his mother. There was bound to be some deep psychological damage from that. One thing was certain: when they got out of here they were both going to need a lot of therapy.

She had come close to asking him earlier what they

would do if following the river turned out to be a dead end, but she decided she didn't want to know the answer to that. She was beyond being scared. Now all she wanted to do was survive. To see the sun again. To feel wind in her face. To enjoy those tiny pleasures that she'd always taken for granted – reading a good book in bed, enjoying a hot cup of coffee first thing in the morning. And music. She missed music. Classic Motown and that 'eighties R&B her dad used to play in the car. She thought of him singing along with Lionel Richie while driving through town and wondered whether she would ever get to experience that again. She went back to concentrating on crawling; thinking of anything else was just too painful.

Ahead of her, Brandon stopped. "What's wrong?" she asked.

"This ledge ends here," he said. "I think we're gonna have to get in the water." He slid down the embankment into the stream below. The water came up to his knees, but he was at least able to stand upright. "Cold," he said.

He reached out a hand and helped her down to the stream. He wasn't kidding about it being cold. Rivers of icy water flooded her shoes and in seconds her feet and calves were painfully numb. They slogged forward, the splashing water almost deafening in the cramped passageway.

"Can we get hypothermia from this?" she asked.

"I don't know," he said.

"What if it gets deeper?"

"I don't know. Just keep moving."

The tunnel kept going, just like all the others they had been through – nothing but jagged rock walls.

Endless. Mind-numbing. Like driving down an interstate in the middle of the night with no destination and
nothing but the lit pavement slicing through the dark.
Her feet were almost completely numb now. Walking
was becoming more difficult, like there was nothing on
the ends of her legs but lifeless lumps of clay.

The flashlight dimmed. Sputtered once, then died
completely, leaving them in complete, utter blackness.

"Fuck, oh *fuck!*" Brandon cried. She could hear him
smacking it against his hands. "No, please. *No!*"

Panic seized Chloe's gut, and she was just about to
reach out and grab hold of Brandon, when she remembered her phone. Still in her backpack. She unhooked
the pack off her shoulders and felt through the outer
zippered pocket. Her hand brushed against the phone
and she pulled it out, filling the chamber with dim, glo-
rious light from the screen. The time read 3:15 AM.

"Oh, thank God," Brandon said. "Thank God."

She opened the flashlight app and handed the phone
to Brandon. It was nowhere near as bright as the real
flashlight had been, but it was better than nothing. It
would have to do.

By now the water was up to their waists. Chloe had
no idea what they would do if it got much deeper. She
couldn't swim, and she cursed herself for never learn-
ing how. She was aware that she was shivering, and
she wondered if it meant hypothermia was setting in.
Brandon was bigger and meatier, and he would last
longer than she would. She thought of what would
happen if she couldn't go on. Would Brandon stay with
her? Would he try to carry her? He was a big guy, and
maybe under normal circumstances he would be able to
manage it. But she was no little snowflake, and Bran-

don – weak from exhaustion and cold – might not be able to hold her.

Her thoughts were interrupted by a gasp from Brandon. "Chloe, be still," he said.

"What is it?" She peered around his shoulder and he pointed toward the ceiling. The whole ceiling was moving, undulating. Fluttering.

Bats. Hundreds of bats. They clung to the ceiling in a mass. Some cleaning themselves. Some sleeping. She could see their tiny eyes reflected as pinpricks of light. A shudder began deep within her, one that had nothing to do with how cold she was, and rippled through her whole body. She hated bats. Her dad had always called them "rats of the sky." And now looking them – black leathery wings and gray mouse-like faces – she understood why.

"Don't make any sudden movements," Brandon whispered. "We don't want to get them stirred up." He inched forward and she followed, trying to stay as quiet in the water as possible, which was hard to do since she could barely feel her feet.

Above them, the bats continued their activities, seemingly oblivious to their presence. They clicked and rustled, some spreading their wings as if stretching. One of them yawned, exposing tiny, needle-like teeth and Chloe felt a wave of revulsion that bordered on nausea.

After an eternity, they were finally away from them. Chloe realized she had been holding her breath, expecting them to swarm the way they did in horror movies, or the way she'd seen in documentaries when they erupted out of a cave. "The bats are good, though, right?" she said, her voice trembling with cold.

"What?"

"The fact that we saw bats. That's good, right? That means we're going the right way. That the opening to the cave is close."

"Yeah," Brandon said. He glanced back at her and she caught a fragment of a smile on his face. "You're right."

But after a while there still was no sign of the mouth of the cave. Just endless walls of rock and freezing water that was now chest high.

Brandon held the phone as high as he could, though Chloe knew his arms must be getting tired. He was shaking as she was from the cold, and she wondered how much longer they would last in this frigid water. She wondered what death would feel like when it finally came. If, as she had read, she would begin to feel warm. Right now it seemed as though she would never be warm again. All she wanted was her worn red cardigan sweater, a hot pumpkin spice latte from Starbucks, and that Karin Slaughter novel she had started a hundred years ago. Sitting in her favorite chair in the apartment. That's all she wanted. Just to be warm.

Ahead of her, Brandon stopped. "Chloe?"

"What?"

He was looking up. "I think we're outside."

She followed his gaze, and the tiny diamonds of stars in the night sky blurred as tears filled her eyes.

EPILOGUE

In the bowels of the earth, where no living beast had ever ventured, it lay in silence. It had been wounded, and now it knew pain. It had been perplexed at the feeling and in the end had retreated to recover. It had known fire before, of course, but never the emotion with which it had been used. Not fear. *Anger.* An elemental feeling it had never encountered from another creature.

It would sleep until it awakened hungry again. But now it had an ample supply of food to last several cycles, and it would not have to hunt for a long while. It would have plenty of time to heal. To plan. To dream. To wonder at this new emotion and devise a way to utilize it in the future.

It had plenty of time. It had always had plenty of time.

ACKNOWLEDGMENTS

No writer works in a vacuum. I'd like to thank my beta reader LaTesha Joiner for making sure my characters stayed consistent and Norma Dossett Tucker for fact-checking all the caving elements for me. I'd also like to thank my wife Tracy for proofreading and copy editing and making sure it all makes sense.

WDO

ABOUT THE AUTHOR

Author and sometime banker Will Overby lives with his wife, a dog, and a menagerie of cats in the rural lakes area of western Kentucky. Between dodging mergers and drafting policies he writes novels. Connect with him on his website, *www.willoverby.com*, on Facebook, or follow him on Twitter (@Will_Overby).